GW00739300

'Is it the hous... or me?'

The fingers tra... deliberately. 'Is there any reason why it can't be both?'

'Would you have still insisted on moving in if I'd been fat and ugly?'

'Without a doubt,' Nicholas replied. 'You, my dear girl, are an added bonus.'

'And one you intend making the most of?'

'Your words, not mine.' Briony knew he was enjoying the situation, playing with her as a cat played with a mouse.

Dear Reader

This month, I would like to ask you to think about the kind of heroine you would like to find in our stories. Do you think she should be sweet and gentle, on the look-out for a man who will be able to care for and nurture her, or should the heroine be able to give as good as she gets, throwing punch for punch, and quite capable of standing up for herself? If you have any opinions on this matter please let us know, so that we can continue to give you the books you want to read!

The Editor

Margaret Mayo was born in the industrial Midlands and began writing fifteen years ago after getting an idea for a romantic short story. It turned into a full-scale novel and she now has over forty novels to her credit. She lives with her husband in a pretty village in Staffordshire and has a grown-up son and daughter. She enjoys setting her books both at home and in exotic locations which she either visits or researches through books from the library.

Recent titles by the same author:

YESTERDAY'S DREAMS

RUTHLESS STRANGER

BY
MARGARET MAYO

MILLS & BOON LIMITED
ETON HOUSE,   18-24 PARADISE ROAD
RICHMOND,   SURREY   TW9 1SR

*First published in Great Britain 1993
by Mills & Boon Limited*

© Margaret Mayo 1993

*Australian copyright 1993
Philippine copyright 1993
This edition 1993*

ISBN 0 263 78177 1

*Set in Times Roman 10 on 11¼ pt.
01-9308-55771 C*

Made and printed in Great Britain

CHAPTER ONE

BRIONY could not believe her eyes when the man pushed rudely past her and marched straight into the house. He had paused only long enough to establish that she was Miss Weston and confirm that he was Nicholas Grant, arriving at the appointed hour to view the property she had for sale.

'Hey, what do you think you're doing?' she yelled after him as he slammed open the living-room door and strode in, his fierce black eyes sweeping the room, taking everything in at a single, critical glance. 'You cannot just walk in here like this. Who the hell do you think you are?'

His eyes blazed at her as he swung around, heavy, jutting brows bristling with the fury that ran through him, but he made no answer. Like a demon he went through each of the rooms in turn, downstairs, upstairs, not speaking to her at all, ignoring her outbursts, her constant attempts to question him, to demand an explanation for his unconventional behaviour. Only once did he pause, and that was to glance at a silver-framed photograph of her stepfather, then he was off again on his breakneck tour.

Briony considered telephoning the police, or at least getting out of the house. She felt afraid, vulnerable, and as Thornton Hall was situated in its own grounds there was no one to hear her shout. Who was this man? What right had he to push his way in like this? Apart from his name she knew nothing about him. Tall—extremely tall; tanned, as though he spent most of his time working

outdoors: coarse black hair, a trifle over-long; a face
that was angular and ruthlessly savage.

He could never be described as handsome and his
fierce scowl seemed to be a permanent part of his features. His nose was aquiline and crooked, as though it
had been broken at one time, and he looked the sort of
man whose temper ran away with him frequently.

His mouth was full, though at this moment, as he
strode from room to room, his lips were compressed into
a tight, grim line. In fact his whole body was rigid with
suppressed anger. Briony wished she knew what had
triggered off this amazing demonic energy that was
carrying him through her house like a whirlwind. She
had the uneasy feeling that it was something to do with
her—though why and for what reason she had no idea.

It was not until he had seen every single room that he
stopped and confronted her. They were back in the hall
with its tiled floor and panelled walls hung with original
oil-paintings of which her stepfather had been particularly proud. 'All right, Miss Briony Weston, I think it
is time you told me exactly who you are.' He had a faint
American accent and a deep-timbred voice that was
unlike any other she had heard.

She stared at him, stunned. 'What do you mean, who
I am? I think it should be me asking you the same
question. You charge in here without permission, you
walk all over the house as though you own the place,
then you have the nerve to ask me who *I* am. *You* are
the intruder, Mr Grant, and I am the one who deserves
an explanation.'

Briony's unusual smoky grey eyes were hot with anger,
her chest heaving, and she stood with arms akimbo, feet
apart. She wasn't small at five feet six inches, yet even
so she felt dwarfed by this threatening stranger.

With her long pale blonde hair hanging loose over her
shoulders she looked much younger than her twenty-six

years. She had intended sweeping it up into a more sophisticated style but this man had turned up earlier than expected and she now felt that it put her at a considerable disadvantage. Nevertheless she stood resolute before him, her eyes never leaving his.

Confronting this man was a frightening sensation; she did not know how dangerous he was, she did not know what crazed thoughts were running through his mind. Black eyes still blazed and he made no attempt at all to explain himself. 'Answer me another question,' he said instead. 'What are you doing in my father's house?'

Briony actually felt her mouth drop open and she stepped back a pace without realising it. This man was certainly full of surprises. 'I beg your pardon?'

'I think you heard.' His tone was abrupt and brooked no hedging.

'Your *father's* house?'

'That's right,' he snapped.

Her chin lifted. 'You've made a mistake, Mr Grant, a very grave mistake. This house does not belong to your father; it belongs to me.'

'Oh, no, it doesn't,' he announced, closing the space between them again so that had he wanted to he could have reached out and touched her.

Several long, tension-packed seconds went by when all they did was eye each other mutinously. Finally Briony spoke. 'For your information this house *used* to belong to my stepfather, Mr James Thornton. When he and my mother died it became mine; it's as simple as that.'

'Oh, no,' he contradicted savagely, 'you're wrong, very wrong; the house belongs to me. James Thornton was my father.'

Astounded by this man's claim, Briony could only stare at him in total disbelief. 'How can James possibly have been your father when he had no children?'

'Is that what he told you?' There was a further blazing fierceness in his eyes.

'More than once.' Her chin was high, her stance belligerent. 'I had no reason to disbelieve him.'

'He was lying,' snorted Nicholas Grant. '*I* am his son and you have no right living in this house. I want you out.'

Briony could not believe what she was hearing. If this man thought he was the rightful heir to Thornton Hall he was certainly labouring under a delusion and she had to find some way of convincing him that he was mistaken. 'How can James Thornton be your father when your name is Grant?' she asked him crisply.

'That's simple,' he told her, his dark eyes ever watchful on here. 'I dropped the Thornton. Grant is my middle name.'

A likely story, thought Briony; he was probably a con man, trying to get the house from her. She must be very careful; she must get him out as quickly as possible. 'I'm sorry, Mr Grant, but unless you can come up with some solid proof as to your identity I shall not believe you. Now would you mind going?' She pulled open the front door and stood back for him to leave.

As she had half expected, he made no attempt to move; instead he walked back into the library and picked up the photograph of her stepfather, studying it intently. 'I have proof,' he said.

'Then let me see it,' returned Briony, her heart thumping within her breast. She neither liked nor trusted this man and was not quite sure how to handle the situation.

'I don't happen to have it with me but I can assure you it does exist.' He took a step across the room towards her.

Briony flinched and edged away, feeling and finding the door-jamb behind her, ready to run should he attempt to touch her.

'You don't have to be afraid,' he announced harshly. 'I have no intention of assaulting you—that isn't my line. What I'm after is the truth. This isn't your house, is it? James wasn't your stepfather. You're a trickster, a gold-digger; you've preyed on the goodwill of an old man and——'

'How dare you?' cut in Briony furiously. 'That isn't the way of things at all. James married my mother; he loved her, they had some happy years together, and if you were his son then you would know.'

'I've been abroad,' he informed her evenly, but although his voice was not quite so abrasive there was still a ruthless hardness in his eyes, and his whole body was tense, fingers curled, as though he was waiting for the opportunity to pounce.

He was dressed in casual, though obviously expensive trousers and jacket in a matching shade of dove-grey, which hid none of his powerful, muscular strength, and Briony certainly did not fancy her chances.

'They were married for six years,' she informed him. 'Twelve months ago they both died in an unfortunate flying accident. *If* you are his son I find it disgusting that in all the time they were married you never once got in touch with him.'

'What I do is my business,' he flashed back, though there was a sudden and surprising shadow in his dark eyes, gone again in an instant, making Briony wonder whether she had imagined it.

'And selling this house is mine,' she snapped. 'Why don't you just go, Mr Grant? You're wasting your time here; you'll get nowhere with me.' Did he really think she'd be gullible enough to believe his story? It was the most absurd thing she had ever heard. How could he be

James's son? Her stepfather had always insisted that he had no children, there were no photographs and she had seen nothing when she went through James's possessions after the tragic accident.

The man put the photograph back in its place but still made no attempt to move towards the front door. 'There's a lot of things you don't know, young lady, but be very sure about this—my daughter and I are both moving in here.'

'You mean you wish to purchase it?' asked Briony, deliberately misunderstanding.

'Damn you, I don't mean that at all and you know it,' he growled.

'It's the only way you'll get your hands on this place,' she retorted. 'It's mine and it's staying that way until it's sold legitimately. Now will you go?'

A hint of a smile curved the corners of his mouth, though no humour lurked in his eyes; they still remained as cold and hard as steel. 'You're sticking it out to the bitter end, are you? I admire your spirit. I will go, yes, but I'll be back, with proof of my identity—have no fear about that. And then we'll see who the house belongs to.'

To Briony's profound relief he headed for the door, but it was short-lived when he paused beside her. She felt menace in every muscle-packed inch of him; even the hairs on the back of her neck prickled and it was all she could do to stop herself moving away. She was determined, though, not to let him see that he intimidated her, and she eyed him resolutely, standing her ground, waiting for him to pass.

He did nothing except hold her gaze and yet, surprisingly, she became suddenly aware of his sensuality. It had not hit her before; she had seen nothing sexual about him at all. Now, for just a second, she felt the full impact, so strong that it stunned her and she held her breath, and then the feeling was gone and he moved away, the front door closing behind him. She guessed she must have imagined it. How could she feel something like that about a man who was trying to turn her out of house and home?

She felt exhausted, as if she'd fought a battle and lost. It was absolutely unbelievable that a strange man could walk in and lay claim to this house, *her* house. She did not believe for one instant that he was James's son. He was lying, he was out to dupe her, he had discovered that she was living alone and that her parents were dead and he was trying to turn the situation to his advantage.

But he had picked on the wrong girl if he thought she would believe him—she wasn't that gullible. She was strong-minded and determined, well able to look after herself. And forewarned was forearmed, so they said. She would be ready for him the next time he came, and she certainly wouldn't allow him to take even one step inside this house; the door would remain firmly locked.

She returned to the library, a long room with oak-panelled walls and matching fitted bookcases, and picked up the photograph of James Thornton. A tall, distinguished gentleman, with snowy-white hair and a long, serious face—and Nicholas Grant looked nothing like him! Apart from their height there was no family resemblance whatsoever, making her even more certain that this younger man had made up the whole story.

Briony's own parents had divorced when she was little and her mother had brought her up single-handed. There had been no other men in her life, even though she was an attractive woman—not until James; and it had done Briony good to see her mother blossom.

They had given up their rented flat and come to live here at Thornton Hall, an impressive stone building set in its own grounds, some of it dating back over six hundred years. It had worked out very well—until the collapse of James's agricultural machinery business. As James's secretary, Briony had known he was having financial difficulties, but she had never dreamt he was in such dire straits. He had never been the same once the company was sold.

Twelve months ago a friend had taken him and Patricia up in his aircraft. Tragically it had developed engine trouble and crashed into a hillside in Wales. No one had survived. Briony had been devastated.

But that was not the end. Her stepfather's financial problems had run over into his private life and after the outstanding bills were paid there was no money left at all. It had shocked her, and she knew her mother had had no idea either that he was virtually penniless. She had looked after Thornton Hall to the best of her ability, but the time had come when the only course left open to her was to sell.

And now this man had turned up claiming that the Hall belonged to him! Where did she go from here? She knew nothing about him except that he was aggressive, pushy, rude and the most hateful person she had ever met. The one man who might know if there was any truth in his claim was her stepfather's solicitor and lifelong friend, Richard Brent.

To Briony's dismay, when she rang his office the next morning she learned that he was on holiday, out of the country for the next two and a half weeks. She was offered the help of his assistant, but she knew that Richard had dealt personally with James Thornton's affairs and if he didn't know of the existence of another will then no one else would. And she knew without a shadow of doubt that Nicholas Grant would return long before the solicitor did.

He came sooner than expected. When she arrived home from work that evening he was waiting for her, leaning nonchalantly against an impressive black Ferrari.

The car looked much more in keeping with the Hall than did her Mini Metro, which she had bought second-hand earlier this year when compelled to sell the Alfa Romeo Spyder James had bought her, together with his Daimler and the BMW he had given her mother.

He watched her gravely as she got out of her car—no greeting, no courtesy smile, nothing. He was dressed in black, his jacket in a very fine, soft, expensive leather. Actually everything about him yelled money. Here was wealth even over and above what his father had once had.

'You've wasted no time,' were her first cold words. Today she had her hair swept up into a French pleat and wore a sophisticated navy suit, bought in more affluent times. With a cream and emerald patterned blouse it suited her well and she felt much more confident than she had the evening before. She felt older and wiser and much happier about confronting him.

A slow smile broke the sternness of his face, but it did no more than lift the corners of his mouth. His eyes— those black, insensitive eyes, narrowed and intent—were as hard and ruthless as before. 'I never believe in wasting time when there's something that I want.'

'And you really think I'll give up this house just like that? To a complete stranger who turns up with some cock-and-bull story that hasn't a thread of truth in it? You're out of your mind, Mr Grant.'

The smile disappeared; his mouth thinned. 'My claim to Thornton Hall is authentic. I thought you'd have checked it out by now.'

'And how am I supposed to do that,' she asked angrily, 'when the man you profess to be your father has always declared he has no offspring? It doesn't make much sense to me. I went through his papers when he died; there was nothing to say he had a son. You're a liar and a cheat and if you don't stop harassing me I shall go to the police. And don't think I don't mean it, because I do. I've heard of your type and they leave a very nasty taste in my mouth.'

Nicholas Grant did not look at all perturbed by her threats, in fact he looked quite amused. 'Perhaps this will change your mind?' He pulled a piece of paper out of his jacket pocket and handed it to her.

Briony could not help noticing that his nails were perfectly manicured, fingers long and square-tipped, hands strong and capable, and where his cuff shot back a thin gold watch adorned his wrist. She wondered whether all these trappings were bought with ill-gotten gains, whether it was his habit to prey on women in distress such as her?

The piece of paper printed in red was a birth certificate. She glanced at it briefly and sceptically. Nicholas Grant; father—James Edward Thornton; mother—Lilian Ellen Thornton, née Chartley.

'You think I'd accept this as proof?' she sneered, thrusting it back at him. 'How do I know it isn't false? Forgeries are made every day. If I'm to believe you then I want much more proof than this.'

Anger tightened every muscle in his face as he took back the single sheet of paper, and his eyes blazed with a new sort of brilliance. 'Then how about this?'

The letter was closely written in James Thornton's familiar hand. Briony frowned as she began to read. James was apparently begging his son's forgiveness, though it did not make clear what had gone wrong between them. However, it was the last paragraph that took Briony's breath away.

I have changed my will in your favour, son. When I die Thornton Hall will be rightfully yours.

Briony looked up at him in astonishment. 'This cannot

be. I saw James's will; he left the house to my mother, and then to me.'

'Are you suggesting this letter is a forgery too?' he asked harshly, every inch of his angular face rigid with anger.

'It does look like James's writing,' she admitted with a tiny lift of her shoulders, 'but I have seen no such will. Maybe he thought about it but didn't actually get around to making one?' The date on the letter was only a few days before the fatal accident.

'My father was not a procrastinator.'

'Then where is the will?' asked Briony coldly. 'It certainly wasn't lodged with his solicitor.'

'It has to be somewhere in the house, of course. I suggest you let me in so that I can look through my father's papers.'

His arrogance annoyed her and she flashed him a look of complete loathing. 'I tell you—there's nothing here. Whatever your father promised he didn't carry out, and as far as I'm concerned that's the end of the matter.'

She turned and walked haughtily towards the house, her back straight, her tread very determined, but when she heard his footsteps behind her she swung about and faced him savagely. 'You're not coming inside,' she spat. 'This house is mine and it's remaining that way until it's officially sold. You're touching nothing.' She looked very beautiful with two spots of high colour in her cheeks, her smoky grey eyes sparking with anger.

'We'll see about that.' His eyes were equally inflamed and the tension in the air was electric.

'You cannot intimidate me, Mr Grant,' she thrust back savagely. 'I'm not afraid of you. As a matter of fact I'm still not entirely sure that I believe you're who you say you are.'

Silence reigned between them for several long, hostile seconds during which they stared fiercely at each other, both hating, both resenting, and then he went on. 'The way I look at it *you* could be the confidence trickster, the one who shouldn't be here. Why should I believe *your* story? What proof have I that your mother married my father? How do I know that you are who you say you are? As you saw from the letter he mentioned that he had remarried, but not that he had a stepdaughter, and no names. How do I know that I can believe you?'

Briony took in a breath of horror. She had never dreamt that he would take this attitude. 'This is crazy,' she gasped, 'an insane situation. Of course my mother married James. I used to work for him, until his company was sold; I actually introduced them, and I have their marriage certificate inside to prove it.'

'Certificates can be forged,' he reminded her, his voice dangerously soft.

Touché, she thought grudgingly.

'I really think we should go indoors and discuss this thing like two rational adults,' he added, 'instead of bawling at each other out here. Losing our tempers will get us nowhere.'

Briony shook her head so violently that one of the pins came out of her hair and its neat French pleat began to disintegrate. Nicholas Grant's eyes were immediately drawn to it and she sensed that he would have liked nothing better than to finish the job.

Most men, she had discovered, preferred women with long hair. She knew that in their eyes it enhanced a woman's femininity, and she felt that they might be oddly intimidated by too short hair, or a woman who wore it severely taken back, like herself. She used it as a defence barrier at the office and it definitely seemed to work. She was treated with far more respect than she would be if she let its silvery length fall over her shoulders.

'You don't agree?' he asked when he finally, and reluctantly, dragged his eyes back to her face.

'I think we've said all that needs to be said,' she answered coolly.

He frowned. 'I don't happen to share your opinion.'

'Then that's just too bad,' she tossed back, 'because that's the way it's going to be. You're not setting one foot inside this house until I have someone else here in authority, such as your father's solicitor.'

'Richard Brent!' he exclaimed in sudden glee. 'Of course. He will be able to settle the whole thing.'

Briony felt herself jolted to a standstill. The fact that he knew the man shredded her last doubts as to his identity. 'Mr Brent is on holiday,' she hissed through unnaturally stiff lips.

'So you have tried to check up?' A quirk was quickly constrained.

'Naturally.'

'And drawn a blank? That is sad. How long will Richard be away?'

Richard! He made it sound as though the man were his friend as well.

'A couple of weeks,' she grudgingly admitted.

He gave a snort of impatience. 'There must surely be someone else who can help in his absence. I have no intention of waiting that long.'

Waiting for what? she wondered apprehensively. To move in, to kick her out, to take the house from her? She took a long, deep breath. 'I cannot believe that you're really serious. There is no other will; I can assure you of that. If there were I would have found it by now.'

'Naturally, but would you have disclosed it?' His eyes were hard upon hers, his tone cutting. 'It certainly wouldn't have been in your best interests, would it?'

'I don't like what you're insinuating,' she snapped.

'Neither do I like what I'm finding out.'

Again, Briony violently shook her head, and the rest of the pins came showering out. Almost at once she realised that she had lost control. They were no longer equals. He was a tough, bloody-minded man and she was a defenceless woman. Defenceless, maybe, but not weak. She jutted her chin and glared. 'I've never been dishonest in my life, Mr Grant. I've had a tough up-bringing, but a just one, and I've learned to look after myself. You don't intimidate me. It's time you left. As far as I'm concerned the conversation is over.'

'Do you know,' he said, and to her amazement he was smiling, 'I never expected to meet such a ferocious female? I quite admire you. On the other hand——' he became suddenly serious again '—I have no intention of letting you win. Rounds one and two to you, but no more.' He held up a warning finger. 'Next time I come it will be for keeps.' He yanked open the door of his car, settled his long length into the seat, fired the engine and with a confident wave—a wave which said, 'See you soon'—and a squeal of tyres, he drove away.

Again Briony was left feeling completely drained. This man sapped her energy; she wasn't sure she'd be strong enough to face him again. For keeps, he had said. What did that mean, that he was going to move in regardless? Kick her out? Take possession? She went cold all over at the very thought.

CHAPTER TWO

BRIONY half expected to find Nicholas Grant lodged outside her house again when she got home from work on Friday evening; it was a relief to discover the drive empty. She had spent all last night and most of the day tossing the situation round and round in her mind and at the end of it all had still come nowhere near to a solution.

She had no choice but to believe that he was James's son, unless both the birth certificate *and* letter were forgeries. If so they were very clever because she felt sure that it was her stepfather's handwriting. And if Nicholas was his son why had James denied his very existence? She searched and searched through her mind for half-forgotten memories, anything James could have said that would confirm Nicholas Grant was truly his own flesh and blood. But she came up with nothing, absolutely nothing.

On Saturday morning she went out shopping and when she got back Nicholas Grant was waiting for her, lounging idly against the front door so that there was no way she could get in without him entering too. Her heart plummeted, but she eyed him bravely as she got out of her car and walked across to him with a loaded bag in each hand. 'I hoped I'd seen the last of you.'

'I told you I'd be back.' He wore a black polo shirt beneath his black leather jacket, giving him a sinister air.

Briony shivered inside. 'You're wasting your time.' She put the heavy bags down but did not reach out her key.

'If I thought that I wouldn't be here. Tell me, how long have you had the Hall on the market?' He looked completely relaxed, as though he was prepared to stand there for however long it took to bring the conversation to a satisfactory conclusion.

The unexpected question caused a frown to furrow Briony's normally smooth brow. 'A long time actually—why?'

'And the reason you're trying to sell?'

Her frown deepened and her tone was sharp as she replied, 'I don't think that's any business of yours.'

'I would suggest it's to make yourself a nice little packet—but it hasn't worked out quite like that, has it?' He still had that insouciant air, his lips quirking, almost as though the whole thing were a joke; yet she knew that he was in deadly earnest. 'You can't sell the place, can you?' he went on. 'People aren't looking for this type of property at the moment. You're stuck with it, your little plot hasn't worked, and it's my guess you're struggling to pay the bills. The job you've got now doesn't pay anywhere near what my father paid you.'

'How do you know that?' Briony's tone was sharp. She did not like to think that he knew so much about her.

'I've been doing a little detective work,' he answered easily. 'Oh, yes, you're right, your mother did marry my father, but what's to say she wasn't in on it too?'

Briony gave a disbelieving gasp. 'You swine!' She lifted her hand with every intention of striking him across the face, but he caught it and held on to it and his face lost its smile, becoming once again harshly, dominantly arrogant.

'Don't ever hit me, Briony Weston, or I'll be compelled to hit you back.'

'Only a coward would strike a woman,' she spat, struggling to free herself.

'Believe me, I'm no coward,' he warned her. 'But neither do I like girls who fight like alley cats. You have the face of an angel—don't ruin the image.'

The face of an angel! No one had ever told her that before, but she wasn't in any way flattered. There was a faint spark of something at the contact, at the feel of those strong-boned fingers about her wrist, but the instant he let her go it was gone, and she glared at him with eyes full of hatred. 'My mother loved James very much, and he loved her. How dare you insinuate that she, that *we* plotted to do your father out of his house?'

'We'll never know, will we?' he said in a voice suddenly quiet.

'One thing I do know,' she snapped, 'is that you're not taking over.' He couldn't do it, could he? He couldn't walk in and commandeer the place? Not until his claim was proven? She had to have some legal rights.

'Assuming that James is your father,' she said, 'you still cannot walk in and take over. If you've denied his existence all these years then I don't see why you should have any claims now. James might have written that letter but he certainly didn't take any action.'

Tension ridged his face; even his voice was tight when he spoke. 'You know nothing about my relationship with my father.'

'Then suppose you tell me,' she taunted.

'Here? Now?' he asked, a caustic edge to his tone.

Briony lifted her shoulders and said grudgingly, 'I suppose you'd better come in.'

An instant smile changed the character of his face; the harsh lines disappeared and he looked almost boyish, and she knew that she had made a grave mistake. But it was too late. Already he had picked up her bags and was waiting expectantly for her to open the door.

As on the first occasion he knew exactly where to go, heading unerringly for the kitchen. He stood watching her as she put away the frozen food, leaning against the wall with that nonchalant ease she was becoming accustomed to. She felt an awareness of him that was unwanted and alien and she flashed him an angry glance. 'Let's go into the sitting-room; I'll finish this lot later.'

'There's no hurry,' he demurred, making no effort to move.

'I happen to think differently,' Briony retorted. 'I have a lot of things to do. I want this conversation over and done with as quickly as possible.'

He gave an easy shrug and allowed her to pass him, following her this time instead of leading, and Briony wasn't sure which she disliked most. She could feel his eyes on her, knew he was watching the way her body moved beneath the lavender wool of her dress. She wasn't quite as slender as she would have liked, her breasts too full, her hips too rounded, but she walked with a natural elegance and was perfectly aware that men's heads turned when she entered a room or walked down a street. She preferred to think it was the silver-blonde of her hair they were admiring.

But this man, she hated him looking at her. She felt surprisingly vulnerable. The masculine smell of him as she brushed past had triggered off something inside her, an unwanted response, an awareness, a knowledge that she could, in different circumstances, find him tremendously exciting.

The sitting-room was light and airy, like all the rooms in the house, with french windows leading out to a terrace. Briony had always found it a relaxing room—until this moment. Nicholas Grant filled it with his unwanted presence and she was too much on edge to even sit down.

She stood at the window, looking out at the wilderness of garden, the overgrown lawns and weed-infested flower-beds; everything far too big for her to keep under control. She had become increasingly conscious of its unkempt appearance and felt sure it had something to do with the property not selling as quickly as she had hoped.

'It looks as though it needs a man to tackle that lot.' Her unwanted companion's voice came quietly over her shoulder. 'What happened to my father's gardener? Did you begrudge paying his wages? Did you want to keep every single penny for yourself?'

Briony moved abruptly away; she needed no reminders of this sort. 'If you've done your research properly then you'll also have discovered that your father died a financially ruined man.'

Nicholas Grant inclined his head. 'I've found out a lot of things I don't like, and you can rest assured that I shall be going into them more deeply. It would appear my father was taken for a ride. No other way could he have lost all his money.'

'Perhaps if you'd been here it wouldn't have happened,' she retorted scathingly.

'It would have made no difference. My father disowned me completely when I was eighteen, and, in case you're wondering, I am now thirty-six.'

'And this is the first time you've been back?' asked Briony incredulously. He actually looked older, no doubt due to the fine lines in his suntanned face and the threads of silver that ran through his black hair.

'That's right.'

'Then I think you should be ashamed of yourself.'

Thick brows slid up. 'My father is the one who maintained the distance. I wrote to him many times in the first couple of years and never once did I receive a reply.'

'You could have come to see him.'

'And got rejected in person?' he asked gruffly. 'No, thank you, I had my pride too. Besides, I'd started a life for myself in America and it had every sign of being successful. I didn't want to give it up.'

'Until you heard that your father had died and you decided that you wanted Thornton Hall?' Briony's tone was derisive.

He shook his head. 'That isn't exactly right.'

'It's what it looks like to me,' she tossed at him. 'What does puzzle me is what took you so long?'

His nostrils flared angrily. 'I actually did not find out until just over a week ago that my father had died—I bumped into an old business acquaintance of his and he naturally spoke of it, assuming that I knew. It was a terrible shock.'

Briony felt like saying it was his own fault for cutting himself out of James's life so completely.

'And to add insult to injury I discover my home is up for sale.' He snorted angrily. 'This is my inheritance, Miss Weston, all that is left to remind me of my father and my childhood, and I'm damn sure that it's not going to some stranger.' His black eyes bored into hers, powerful and threatening. 'I've told my daughter so much about it; we're both looking forward to moving in.'

Briony felt her hackles rise. He sounded so sure of himself. How she would like to kick him right out of this house. He was a swine and she hated him. 'What's happened to your wife?' she asked tersely. 'Where is she?'

'I never married,' he said, his bark of laughter harsh and self-derogatory. 'Sit down and I'll tell you about it. At the age of eighteen I fell in love with a beautiful girl— Leonora was her name, Leonora Cameron. Have you heard of the Camerons?'

'No, I haven't,' Briony admitted, wondering why he thought she might have done.

'Nor had I. But apparently it was a cardinal sin falling for this lovely creature. Her family and ours, the Thorntons, were sworn enemies. A feud had been going on for generations, rearing its ugly head every decade or so when something happened to offend one of the families. Me wanting to marry Leonora was enough to start it all off again.'

'You were told to keep away from her?'

'That's right,' he said, 'and telling me something like that was like holding a red rag to a bull. It was the first time in my life I'd ever defied my father, but I felt that I was man enough to know my own mind. Eighteen and knew it all, that was me.'

'So what happened?' asked Briony, interested despite herself. It was an intriguing tale; James had not breathed one word about any of this. He had eradicated every single memory of his son from his life.

'Rather than give each other up we ran away together. Leonora's family were putting her under similar pressure. It seemed the exciting thing to do to go to America. We settled in Houston and I got a job working on the oil-rigs; it paid excellent money and gave us a good start. We were able to afford a decent apartment, but Leonora wasn't happy about the long hours I worked and the time I spent away from home; she even changed her mind about wanting to get married. When she discovered she was pregnant I thought it would make a difference, but it didn't. When the baby was born she dumped her unceremoniously on me, saying, "You got us into this mess; you can look after her. I've had enough." I was completely knocked out; I had no idea she felt so strongly.'

'And that was it, the end of your relationship? You've not seen her since?' asked Briony.

'Not once.'

'You didn't go after her?'

'No.' He shook his head emphatically. 'In all honesty my own feelings for her had waned too; as a matter of fact I don't think I ever truly loved her, and besides, I quite liked living in America. It was so different from England, so exciting. I was getting on well, earning a lot of money; I really loved it.'

'And you never thought about coming back to see your father, once you and Leonora had split up? You had every reason then to make amends. Don't you think he'd have liked to see his granddaughter, or at least to have known that he'd got one?'

A shadow crossed his face. 'I thought of it many times, I was on the verge of it many times, but then I thought of all my unanswered letters. He'd got my address. If he'd wanted he could have gotten in touch with me.'

'He did,' Briony reminded him.

Nicholas nodded. 'I've read that letter frequently, believe me, but it wasn't that easy. I wanted to come back when he offered the olive branch. I'd even been thinking about it before then, but I was going through a critical time—I'd bought a piece of land some years back that proved to be rich in oil and we were having a few problems. I needed to keep my eye on things. By the time I could safely get away it was too late,' he added gruffly.

'You could at least have written or telephoned, given him some idea that you were planning a visit.'

'I wanted to, believe me,' he answered wearily. 'It was just so hard after all that time. I thought it best I came in person. I could sure use a drink; do you have any whisky?'

Briony stood up. 'There's some of your father's left.'

He rose too. 'If it's still kept in the same place then I know where it is; I'll help myself.'

'How do I know whether it's in the same place as eighteen years ago?' she asked sharply and resentfully.

'I'll get it.' As far as she was concerned this was still legally her house and he was an intruder, uninvited and unwanted, and had no right making himself so much at home.

She did not feel sorry for him; on the contrary it was James she felt sorry for. The older man had finally chosen to try and heal the rift and all Nicholas had done was ignore his appeal. It served him right that he was too late, and she was darned sure that she was not going to give up this house without a jolly good fight.

When she returned to the room with the half-full bottle of Glenfiddich and a crystal glass she set them noisily on the mahogany-inlaid table beside him. '*Now* you can help yourself,' she remarked crisply.

He gave her a quizzical look from beneath black brows but said nothing, pouring a generous measure and downing it in one swallow. 'That's better,' he said, re-charging the glass but leaving it on the table, settling back again in his chair and eyeing Briony steadily. 'So what's the position now? Am I going to be allowed back into my own home?' He looked absolutely relaxed, sitting well back, hands on the arms, one ankle resting on the other knee, as though he was prepared to stay there for a long time.

'Not while I have breath in my body,' she told him, her eyes cool on his. She might have known it was a mistake inviting him inside. He looked as though it would take a bomb to get him out again. 'It's a very convincing story you've told me, and I really have no choice but to believe it, but the truth of the matter is that James left this house to me—and I don't care to move out for his estranged son.'

'There is the question of the other will,' he reminded her harshly, a muscle suddenly tensing in his hard-boned jaw.

'Which might never have been made out,' she rasped.

'A search has to be made.'

Briony hissed her impatience. 'As I said before, I've already gone through James's papers. There's nothing there, I assure you.'

'I'd like to look for myself.'

Angrily she shook her head, her cheeks high with unusual colour. 'I will not allow a perfect stranger to invade my privacy in such a way.'

Nicholas let out a bellow. '*Your* privacy—I like that. This is *my* home; you are the outsider.'

'No, I am not,' she riposted. 'You are the one who walked out on it. You gave up all your rights to this place.'

'Not according to my father,' he reminded her. 'I went along to see Richard Brent's stand-in this morning. He sees no reason why I shouldn't move in until the matter is resolved. It is my home as much as yours, after all; in fact even more so.'

'*What*?' Briony could not believe what she was hearing. 'He said that to you?'

'He did indeed.'

'He has no right,' she retorted sharply. 'He should wait for Mr Brent's return; he's the only one who knows your father intimately enough to be able to deal with this matter, in fact the only one who'll know whether you are who you say you are. Where are you living now? What's wrong with staying there?'

His eyes watched her closely, noting her anger, but remaining completely unmoved by it. 'In a hotel, but I hate them; I much prefer my own home. I cannot describe my feelings when I discovered Thornton Hall was up for sale. To think I might have been too late.'

'You were,' Briony tossed back caustically. 'Twelve months too late.'

His mouth firmed as her shaft hit home, but he said nothing.

'So why didn't you make yourself known when you saw the sale notice?' she demanded. 'Why did you make an appointment to view?'

'Believe me, I did knock; I almost banged the door down. Obviously you were out. I decided my best chance was to go through the correct channels.'

'I'm sorry you were disappointed,' she said caustically.

'I bet you are,' he growled. 'But the position is that my daughter and I are moving in whether you like it or not.' There was no hint of a smile on his harshly angular face; his gaze was direct, his attention on her.

'Over my dead body,' she expostulated.

He sighed heavily. 'Can't you see that it's the most sensible solution all round? We need to sort this thing out, and this place is easily big enough to hold the three of us.'

Briony shook her head wildly, her heart clamouring within her breast. 'It's a preposterous suggestion. How can I share with a complete stranger? You've out of your mind.'

'We would have a chaperon, if it's propriety that's bothering you.'

'Your daughter?' queried Briony with contempt. 'A mere child?'

He lifted his shoulders. 'It *is* a third person.'

She shook her head in total disbelief. 'You're insane. This is a crazy situation—I'm going to see this solicitor myself. He had no right agreeing to such a proposition.'

Nicholas smiled humourlessly. 'He really had no choice.'

'Meaning you talked him into it?' The nerve of this man. She had never met anyone like him. Could he really be James's son? James had been so gentle, so kind, nothing like this ruthless stranger who seemed determined to make her life hell.

'Something like that,' he confessed with an easy shrug. 'And the office is closed now until Monday so I'm afraid there's not a thing you can do about it.'

'Legally the house is mine,' she returned through gritted teeth.

'And I say that it's legally mine. A stalemate affair, don't you agree? And until it's sorted we're both entitled to live here.'

Briony shook her head, anger seething inside her. What could she do? What could she say? He had an answer for everything and his mind was made up. Short of keeping all the doors locked and bolted, she had no choice. Perhaps she ought to do that?

'I wouldn't try it.'

She looked at him startled, unable to believe that he had read her thoughts as clearly as if she had spoken the words aloud.

'I wouldn't be averse to breaking a window.'

'I don't suppose you would be,' she said bitterly. 'What are your plans? Is it your intention to make your home here in England, or get me out of the house and then sell it yourself and go back to the States?'

'Sell it? Never!' he roared. 'This is my home, my inheritance; I've surely made that clear. It belongs to the Thorntons and I intend to see that it remains that way.'

Briony found his sentiments particularly galling. 'For eighteen years you've stayed away,' she cried furiously, 'for eighteen years you've called yourself Grant, and now you have the audacity to say that this place is your home, your inheritance. Damn you, Nicholas Grant, you're the lowest of the low and I hate your guts. Stay if you must, but only until Richard Brent returns and clears the matter up. We'll see who's in the right then. I loved James as if he were my own father, which is more than can be said for you.'

His lips thinned until they were almost invisible. 'I have always loved my father.'

'Then you had a strange way of showing it,' she spat. 'Are you planning to sell up in America and start again here? In case you'd forgotten, there are no oil-rigs in Staffordshire.'

'My thoughts were that I would take over my father's company,' he told her easily. 'I had no idea that it had gone the way it had. It is something I intend looking into with all speed. I shall very probably buy it back again. I hate to think of it being in someone else's hands.'

He sipped his whisky, savouring the taste, holding the glass up to the light to appraise the clear pale amber contents, finally putting it down again and looking at her. 'And I want you to take the house off the market right now. It shall never be sold, not in my lifetime.'

There was a finality to his voice that sent Briony's temper rising. 'It remains to be seen whether the house belongs to you or me. As far as I'm concerned at this moment in time it belongs to me and it's going to stay up for sale. As a matter of fact I've got someone coming to look at it in the morning. They seem very keen.'

His eyes darkened angrily. 'Then I suggest you give them a ring right now and explain that the house is no longer for sale.' He pushed himself to his feet and crossed to her chair, towering menacingly, his fingers curled into his palms as though he was having the greatest difficulty keeping his hands off her.

Briony rose too, then wished she hadn't when she almost cannoned into him. It was there again, that intense sexuality that took her unawares. She moved quickly away, breathing in deeply, trying to remain calm, telling herself that she was imagining this reaction.

'Why should I?' she protested crossly. 'Why should I do what you say? You haven't altered one little bit, have you? You're still the arrogant eighteen-year-old who wanted his own way, who didn't care who he hurt in the process. I'm changing nothing.'

Again his jaw tightened, but before he could speak she went on, 'As I can see I have no chance of stopping you moving in I fully intend drawing up a set of ground rules. So God help you or your daughter if you fall foul of them.'

His hands touched her shoulders and she flinched, expecting him to hurt, amazed when his touch was as soft as a caress. 'I don't think it will be as hard as you imagine. With a bit of co-operation it could work very well.'

'Co-operation?' Briony jerked free, trying to ignore the tingle of electricity that ran through her. 'I have no intention at all of putting *myself* out. This is your problem, Mr Grant, not mine. You two keep yourselves to yourselves and I keep to myself. Is that clear?'

'Perfectly.' His voice was serious, but his lips twitched and Briony felt like taking a swipe at him, only the fact that she knew who would come off worst stopping her. 'And if we're to live together I think you should call me Nicholas,' he added. 'Mr Grant's rather formal, don't you agree?'

'I'm amazed you're not reverting to Thornton,' she answered scathingly.

'Oh, believe me, I shall, but it's early days yet. I'll settle in first.' He walked out of the room and headed for the front door. 'I'll see you later,' he said with a sudden grin. 'I think this should prove quite an interesting exercise.'

Briony did not smile in response; she was furious. It was all happening against her will; she'd been given no choice—not when one of Richard Brent's fellow solicitors had apparently given his approval. What sort of persuasive powers had Nicholas Grant used? She had no doubt he could be very charming when he wanted. He probably almost always got his own way. God, she hated the man.

Nevertheless he still left his dynamic, crackling presence behind; it was there all about her, in the very air that she breathed, and she knew without a doubt that the next couple of weeks were going to be sheer hell. He was not the type of man you could ignore. She had to be strong; she could not allow the situation to be turned to his advantage. She had to make the rules and insist that he stick to them.

She could not understand why James had never said anything about Nicholas. The feud between the two families must have been very strong for the older man to cut his son out of his life so completely. And how had he felt when he had finally written after all those years and got no reply? It was so sad.

There was also the question of Paul. Dear Paul, she had almost forgotten him in the trauma of the last few days. How would he take all this? He certainly wouldn't be happy when he discovered that his girlfriend had a man living in the house with her. He didn't like her being here alone at the best of times. On the other hand he had never suggested moving in himself!

Returning to the kitchen, she put the rest of her shopping away and filled the kettle to make herself a drink, but before it had even boiled the doorbell rang. Surely he couldn't be back so soon? She gave an inward groan and her feet felt as heavy as lead as she walked along the tiled hall and pulled open the heavy oak door.

At first she could not believe what she saw. Nicholas Grant, yes, but the girl with him was no child as she expected; she was grown-up, a teenager as tall as herself, pretty if her lips weren't so petulant or her blue eyes so resentful. After a first curious look at Briony she cast her eyes downwards and it was clear by her demeanour that she was as unhappy about the situation as Briony herself. Only Nicholas was smiling.

CHAPTER THREE

'BRIONY,' said Nicholas Grant formally. 'I'd like to introduce my daughter, Josephine. Jojo, this is Miss Weston.'

The girl looked up, but did not speak, and when Briony held out her hand she ignored it. Briony gave a mental shrug. In fact it helped that the girl wasn't happy about coming here. Perhaps Nicholas might change his mind.

Several suitcases stood beside them and he said sharply to his daughter, obviously annoyed by her attitude, 'We'd best get these inside.'

Obediently she picked up two of the smaller ones and followed him. Briony stood back and watched as they mounted the stairs. Despite the fact that the girl had golden-blonde hair, they were strikingly similar—the same build, the same strongly shaped faces—and Briony guessed that in another year she would be almost as tall as her father.

She returned to the kitchen and as she sat drinking her coffee Briony wondered about the changes that were being made to her life. For the last twelve months she had had the house to herself, but she had never been lonely and she resented this intrusion on her privacy. Picking up the notepad she always kept in the kitchen drawer, Briony began to formulate a list of rules. Kitchen to be left clean and tidy at all times; own food to be supplied—she would clean out one of the cupboards and allocate space in the fridge and freezer; certain rooms to be out of bounds—she would have to work out which;

washing not to be done weekends—which was when she did her own.

'Is all this necessary?'

Briony jumped as Nicholas Grant's scathing voice came over her shoulder. 'Goodness, do you always walk around so quietly?'

'You were engrossed—and such petty rules. What do you mean, own food? Are you suggesting we cook and eat separately?'

'Most definitely I am,' returned Briony firmly. 'I didn't ask for any of this and I insist on my own privacy. Why didn't you tell me your daughter was a teenager, and by the look of it a very rebellious one? I got the impression that she was a mere child.'

'Actually Jojo didn't want to leave America,' he announced, a sudden tightening to his jaw. 'She'll come round, don't worry about her.'

'Believe me I shan't,' she told him, wishing he would move away. 'I have no intention of losing sleep over either of you. I just hope, though, that she's not going to be a nuisance and bring careless, thoughtless friends to the house. I don't want any of James's prized collection of Lalique glass getting broken.'

'Some are already missing,' he pointed out coolly.

Briony was surprised he had noticed and she nodded, her face regretful. 'I had to sell them to pay off bills when he died, a lot of other items as well.'

'Things were that bad?' He frowned.

'I'm afraid so.'

His mouth tightened and for a few seconds his thoughts were far away. Briony took the opportunity to slide off her stool and move to the other side of the kitchen. It was like being in a vacuum: he drew all the air out of her, leaving her slightly breathless and definitely puzzled by her reaction.

He was the most overpowering man she had ever met, she disliked him intensely, and yet... there was something about him that caused these unwanted feelings whenever he was near. It was going to be sheer hell having him in the same house.

'Jojo won't be any problem,' he told her. 'She's a good girl, and once she gets used to living here I'm sure you'll be the best of friends. After all, there can't be more than a year or two difference in your ages.'

Briony threw him a look of disgust. 'I'm twenty-six and feel a whole lot older. The responsibilities I've had forced on me this last year have taught me a lot.'

'I should have been here,' he muttered through tight lips.

'You're telling me,' she returned sharply.

'There's no need to rub it in,' he growled, 'and I see no reason why everything can't be worked out amicably.'

'Amicably?' she echoed. 'With a complete stranger in the house, and a child who definitely doesn't want to be here? I can see it being a whole load of fun.'

'I'm not a child.' Josephine appeared from the side of the doorway, where she had obviously been standing listening. 'But you're right: I don't want to live in this mausoleum. I hate it, and I hate you, Nick, for bringing me here. I want to go back home.'

'This is your home now, young lady, and you'd be as well to remember it,' Nicholas told her sharply.

Briony listened in horror. He was speaking as though his moving in was a permanent arrangement, as though he was quite confident the house would be his and she would be the one kicked out into the cold.

'There are obviously things that need to be sorted out,' said Nicholas tersely. 'However, I don't see any problem in the long run. There is no doubt that this house is mine—is ours, in fact. Obviously I won't be so callous as to kick Miss Weston out, but——'

'You're damn right you won't,' shot Briony fiercely. 'In fact I shall fight you every inch of the way and I shall certainly have no compunction about kicking *you* out.' Her heart-rate increased and she wished with all her might that she was a man and could settle this battle with her fists. He had no right treating her like this, none at all. James had been so different, so kind, so paternal. If he knew what his son was doing he would turn in his grave.

Nicholas's eyes on hers were cold and relentless. 'This is a matter that will be settled legally. It has nothing to do with what I wish or what you wish. It is my father's wishes that are in question. And I am totally convinced that there is another will. He would never have written that letter otherwise.'

'And I've no doubt you intend turning the house upside-down until you find it,' she returned aggressively. The situation grew worse by the minute; she would never have a moment's peace until this matter was resolved, and maybe not even then if it turned out that the house was legally his. Even if it wasn't he would still fight her—he would take her to court; he would contest the will. It was plain that once Nicholas Grant set his mind on something he went all out to get it, nothing or no one stopping him.

'That's about the score,' he answered easily, and to his daughter, 'Have you unpacked?'

Josephine shook her head, her eyes sullen and resentful.

'Then I suggest you get on with it.'

'I'm hungry,' the girl grumbled.

'We'll eat when you've finished.'

Reluctantly, and after flashing Briony another spiteful, almost malevolent glance, the young girl flounced out of the room. It seemed as though she was saying all of this was Briony's fault.

'Jojo's not usually so impertinent,' said Nicholas, 'and she probably is hungry—I'm starving, myself. What have you got to eat?'

Start as you mean to go on, Briony reminded herself grimly. Don't give way, not an inch. 'Nothing—at least nothing for you.' She stared right back into the blackness of his eyes. He had long, thick lashes and the whites were clear. They were beautiful eyes, much too nice for a man, and they seemed oddly out of place in the harshness of his face. 'You'll either have to eat out or go shopping, and while you're away I'll find you space in the cupboards.'

She was unprepared for his bellow of anger. 'Are you so petty-minded that you begrudge us one meal?'

'One can mount up to two to three to four, and before you know it I'll be providing and cooking all your meals,' she told him coldly.

'I'll pay for the groceries.'

'And we'll be like one happy family? Is that what you're suggesting?' Her voice filled with scorn. 'No, thank you, that's not part of the agreement. We are two separate entities. You've forced yourself on me and I don't seem to have much choice about it, but I am not doing one single thing for you, nor providing anything for you—you can rest assured about that. Call me what you like—narrow-minded, mean, petty, bigoted, or whatever—I don't care. It's the way things are going to be.'

The air around them was charged with tension. Briony had never had to stand up to anyone like Nicholas Grant before, but strangely she found herself actually enjoying the situation. It was a battle of wills, and she was determined that he was not going to win.

'You sound as though you mean it.' His tone was level, but Briony could sense the very real anger simmering inside him. It actually lit a flare in his eyes which sparked across the kitchen.

She drew in a breath. 'I do.'

'From whom did you inherit your stubborn streak—your mother or your father?'

'I cannot remember my father,' Briony declared. 'He walked out when I was three years old. Maybe I am like him, I don't know. My mother was a very gentle, caring person, and to be quite honest I've never been put in this sort of situation before.'

'You can't cope,' he jeered.

'I didn't say that,' she retorted sharply.

'But you're still serious about us eating out?'

Briony nodded.

'Have you had your own lunch?'

'Not yet.'

'Then perhaps you'd like to join us?'

She could not believe that he meant it, not after all she had said. It was like turning the other cheek, and she was sure this was not like him. Admittedly she did not know him at all well yet, but from what little she had seen he would not make an offer like this unless it was to his advantage. She eyed him coldly. 'No, thanks, I have other things to do.'

'Like emptying cupboards to make space for our food?' he shot back with sudden venom.

'If you don't like the situation then you know what you can do,' Briony returned with equal acrimony.

'Oh, no, I'm not getting out of here.' His eyes were sharp on hers. 'This is my home, this is where I intend to stay.'

Her chin jutted with characteristic firmness. 'We'll see about that when Richard Brent gets back.'

'A lot can happen before then,' he answered darkly.

It sounded like a threat, and actually he looked very intimidating—a devilish stranger dressed all in black, insinuating himself determinedly and forcefully into her life. Briony felt her skin crawl.

When they had gone she did not feel like eating. She sat down again instead and pondered her fate. She wished her mother and James were still alive. She wished she did not have to cope with any of this. She wished James had lodged a will with Richard Brent if he really had intended Nicholas to inherit Thornton Hall. Everything was such a mess. If things did turn out in Nicholas's favour what would happen to her? Where would she live? She would have no money to buy another place. It would mean rented accommodation, and she was not sure that she would like that after living in this gracious old house for so long.

Two hours went by before they returned. She had eaten a sandwich, shuffled things around in the kitchen cupboards, and was busy polishing the Regency mahogany sideboard in the hall when she heard his car on the drive.

Both Nicholas and his daughter were loaded with bulging bags, but Briony did not follow them through into the kitchen even though she was curious to see what he had bought. She carried on cleaning and when Josephine walked through to go up to her room, ignoring Briony completely, she muttered under her breath and polished all the harder.

'Couldn't you do with a woman to give you a hand with all that?' asked Nicholas a few minutes later. 'Hadn't my father used to have a daily?'

Again he had come up on her silently. Briony flashed him a look of scorn. 'Where would I find money to pay a cleaner? In any case, I don't do the whole house every week, only the rooms I use.' She had put dust-covers over most of the furniture in the others. 'Naturally I shall expect you or your daughter to keep clean whichever rooms you take over.'

'Naturally,' he answered, but there was mockery rather than seriousness in his voice and Briony looked at him sharply.

'I mean it,' she spat. 'I'm not going to clean up after you. I have little enough spare time as it is. Make sure your daughter knows that as well.'

He looked surprised by the harshness of her tone. 'We always had a maid in Houston; Jojo didn't have to do anything.'

'Then it's a good time for her to learn,' shot back Briony fiercely. 'I'll show her where the cleaning materials are kept.'

'Is this how you spend all your Saturdays?'

He looked as though he was prepared to stand talking for a long time. Briony felt impatience rise inside her and she rubbed unnecessarily hard at the legs of a chair. She did not want to be friends with him; she did not want this chumminess; she wanted to be left strictly alone. 'Mostly.'

'Shouldn't a girl your age be out having fun? It's wrong to turn yourself into a household drudge.'

'I don't have much other choice, do I?' she snapped. 'And I'm quite happy doing it—at least, I was until you came on the scene. Would you mind leaving me alone to get on with it?'

'Yes, I would mind,' he answered, plucking the duster from her. 'This isn't a very auspicious start to our friendship, is it?'

'Friendship?' echoed Briony indignantly, standing to face him, pushing her hair back off her face. She felt hot and bothered and not the least in the mood for such a conversation. 'You can forget that; I intend to live my life as though you're not here.'

'Don't you think that will be impossible?' His black eyes were steady on hers, his thumbs hooked into his belt, his whole stance relaxed.

'Only if you make it so,' she riposted. 'If we both abide by the rules then there should be no problem.'

'Ah, yes, the rules.' The corners of his mouth quivered. 'I always say that rules are made to be broken. Life's no fun otherwise.'

'It's what I might expect from you,' thrust Briony acidly. 'You rebelled against your father, you probably rebel against the whole of society, and your daughter's following the same pattern.'

'Let's leave Jojo out of this.' Anger tightened the muscles in his face, drawing the skin tautly over angular cheekbones. 'It was very traumatic for her leaving the only home she's ever known. It will take a while for her to adjust.'

Briony privately thought he was making excuses for his daughter. The way the girl had ignored her and bounced upstairs had nothing to do with being upset—it was pure bad manners. She snatched the duster out of his hand. 'Thank you, I've finished in here now.' And she walked away without another word.

'Briony.'

She stopped and turned reluctantly, her eyes resentful, and it flashed through her mind that she was behaving exactly like his daughter.

'It isn't going to work, you shutting me out like this.'

She lifted her shoulders. 'I'm sorry, but that's the way it's going to be. As far as I'm concerned this is still my home and you're not welcome.'

'And as far as I'm concerned this is *my* home and you are the intruder.'

Briony stiffened. 'I still have a copy of your father's will, in which my mother and I inherited everything.'

'A will revoked by his later one.'

'A will never found,' she retorted firmly, 'probably never even penned. It's all wishful thinking on your part.'

'That's nonsense, Briony, and you know it.' His tone was sharp with anger. 'Unless you know something I don't?' His eyes were narrowed and watchful on hers.

'Of course not,' she snapped. 'If I had found another will I would most definitely have handed it to Mr Brent.'

'Even if it meant bad news for yourself?'

Briony inclined her head.

'Such honesty,' he mocked and it was clear he did not believe her. 'Time alone will tell whether you're speaking the truth. The will has to be somewhere and I'll most definitely find it. Meanwhile the logical solution is for us to become friends. It's pointless being at loggerheads all the time.'

'Never!' she cried. 'I could never become friends with you. I do not condone your attitude, not one little bit. As far as I'm concerned, the less I see of you the better.'

His lips thinned and his eyes flashed, but his tone was level when he spoke. 'Tell me, Briony, have you a boyfriend? Is he the reason you're being so unsympathetic?'

His sudden change of subject took her by surprise and she frowned as she nodded. 'Yes, I do actually, but he has nothing to do with my attitude towards you.'

He walked towards her, smiling suddenly. 'I imagine he's not very happy at the prospect of another man in the house?'

'He doesn't know.'

Nicholas frowned his surprise, as if wondering what sort of a relationship they had that she had not told him what was happening.

'He's away at a seminar,' she explained.

'Ah, I see,' he said with a nod. 'What do you think his reaction will be? Will he object to me living with you?'

'What do you think?' asked Briony sharply.

He lifted his shoulders in an indifferent shrug. 'It depends on the type of person he is. Is he understanding or jealous? Reasonable or prejudiced?'

'I don't know,' answered Briony sharply. 'I've never given him any reason to be jealous. He's a good man, kind and considerate; I've never had an argument with him.'

Black brows slid up. 'He sounds like a paragon of virtue. How long have you been going out with him?'

Briony was reluctant to answer, but, as the silence lengthened, and it became clear he would wait for ever if necessary, she said, 'Just over six years.'

'My God,' he said in surprise, 'and you haven't got married or even engaged yet? If you ask me, he's not worth knowing.'

'How dare you?' Briony's eyes flashed. 'He's a wonderful man and I love him dearly.'

'He sounds wonderful,' came the sardonic reply. 'In my opinion any man who keeps a girl hanging around that long is either a selfish bastard or a wimp.'

Briony gasped. 'Paul is neither; I resent that remark. You have no right making such a judgement when you don't know him.'

'And when shall I have the pleasure of meeting this— man you defend so heatedly?'

His slight pause over the word man had Briony's hackles rising even higher. 'Never, if I can help it,' she spat fiercely. 'I can just imagine the sort of conversation you'd have with him.'

The corners of his mouth lifted. 'Does he come here often—when he's not away on a seminar, that is? Does he—er—sleep here?'

'Trust you to think of something like that.' Briony felt her cheeks flame with anger, her whole body so tense she felt it would snap in two if he so much as touched her. 'Or is it that you're judging me by your own standards? Is that the sort of thing you would do?'

'Touchy, aren't we?' Still he looked amused. 'You know what they say about people who protest too much? But if you don't want to answer, then far be it from me to insist. What you do is your own affair.'

Meaning he thought that she did sleep with Paul. 'As a matter of fact Paul never has stayed here,' she told him coldly and defensively.

'He's never even suggested it?'

'Of course he has,' she said, though he hadn't, and it had sometimes hurt her that he'd never shown much interest in the physical side of their relationship. 'It was me who said no.'

'Doesn't that tell you something?'

She frowned. 'What do you mean?'

'If you really loved the guy you'd want to sleep with him, and what could be more romantic than making love in a four-poster bed? Tut, tut, Briony. I'm disappointed in you.'

So he knew which bedroom she slept in! On his whistle-stop tour of the house he had mentally noted which one was hers. 'You're a swine and I hate you,' she spat. 'What Paul and I do is no concern of yours.'

'I should hate you to waste your life on someone unworthy of you,' he remarked levelly. 'If you ask me I don't think either of you are in love; I think you've settled into a relationship that isn't worth a dime. I think you should put an end to it right now.'

'Oh, you do, do you?' Briony tossed her hair back off her face and looked at him coldly. 'I didn't realise you were an expert on these sorts of things. Thank you for the advice, but I don't think I shall be taking it. I'm quite capable of making up my own mind.'

Nicholas lifted his shoulders. 'It's your prerogative, honey. Who am I to stop you ruining your life? What does he do, this man of yours, that takes him away from you for long periods at a time?'

She eyed him testily. 'He's in insurance, as a matter of fact; not that I think it's any business of yours.'

His eyes rolled heavenwards. 'No wonder he's as dull as ditch-water. Couldn't you have picked a guy with a more exciting job?'

'I didn't choose Paul because of what he did,' she thrust at him savagely. 'It's immaterial. It's the sort of person he is that I'm interested in—and I happen to think he's very nice.'

'Nice? *Nice*?' he repeated caustically. 'What sort of a word is that? A piece of music can be nice, a meal can be nice; not a person—it's no description at all. It actually suggests what I said in the first place—a wimp.'

Briony shook her head furiously. 'I've had enough of this. Paul will be back soon and then you can see for yourself that he's not as weak-minded as you're suggesting. And when I tell him what sort of a swine you are he'll lose no time in kicking you out.'

Brows rose. 'A toughie, eh? Not the usual run-of-the-mill insurance salesman? This sounds interesting; I'm sure looking forward to meeting him.'

'I wouldn't be too keen if I were you,' she returned, hanging on to her temper by a very thin thread.

'You think he'll pose a threat?'

Looking at Nicholas, hard muscle packed into a big, powerful body, she knew that physically Paul stood no chance at all, but on a mental level then it was a different story altogether. Paul was quick-witted and clever and would surely be able to run rings round this man who she felt sure thought brawn was better than brains any day. 'It will be interesting to see what happens.'

'I agree with you, extremely interesting,' he said with a slow smile. 'What are you going to do with the rest of the day?'

Again another lightning change of subject that took her by surprise. 'I'm going out,' she said tersely. It was a spur-of-the-moment decision, but the idea of spending another eight hours in this man's company was not her idea of fun at all.

'What will lover-boy have to say about that? Won't he expect you to sit at home and meekly wait for him?'

'Paul is not my keeper,' she returned furiously.

'I'm glad to hear it. Why don't you cancel and let me take you out instead?'

Briony could scarcely believe his audacity. 'You have a nerve, Mr Grant. Haven't I made it clear that I want our two lives to remain separate?'

'Extremely clear, but it's a pity; I find you a very attractive young woman. Won't you change your mind?'

He found her attractive! Briony groaned inwardly. This compounded the issue without a doubt, and the fact that her body responded to his against her will made it doubly dangerous. Her mind did not warm to him—not at all— but there was something inside her that certainly overrode every sensible decision she wished to make. She swung away. 'Not ever.'

This time he let her go and as she entered the kitchen she heard him taking the stairs two at a time. He was certainly a man full of surprises. First he had accused her of being a trickster, of worming her way into James Thornton's heart to get her hands on his property—he had virtually said he wanted her out of the house—now he was saying he found her attractive! Where did he intend to go from here?

She put her duster and polish away and went up to her own bedroom. She could faintly hear Nicholas and his daughter talking and she paused at the top of the stairs when the girl's voice rose in sudden anger. 'You can't make me stay. I hate this house—it's too big and too quiet; there's nothing to do, nowhere to go.'

'You'll make friends once you start college.'

'That's another thing—I don't want to go back to school. I'm sixteen—I want to get a job; I want to earn some money. You've no idea what it's been like since you cut my allowance.'

'I'm doing it for your own good, young lady. It's my belief I did you no favours in the first place by being so generous,' Nicholas told her firmly. 'Perhaps now you'll learn to appreciate the value of money. But whatever you do to earn yourself some extra it will be during your vacations or at weekends, certainly not at the expense of your education.'

'It's not fair,' wailed Josephine.

'I'm not happy about the situation either,' he answered, 'but it's something we have to put up with for the time being.'

'That woman has no right living in your house.'

About to proceed to her own room, Briony paused when she heard herself being talked about.

'It wouldn't be so bad if *she* weren't here, if *she* weren't lording it over the place as though it belongs to her,' Josephine went on. 'I don't intend doing anything she asks, and the sooner you get her out of here the better. This is your house, after all. We'll be able to have parties and really live it up like we did in Houston and then it might be worthwhile living again.'

Briony expected Nicholas to chastise his daughter but instead he said calmly, 'I agree the house is rightfully mine, and I'm working on Miss Weston—don't worry your pretty head about her. I have no intention of letting it go out of the Thornton family.'

Working on her! Briony gasped so loudly it was a wonder they didn't hear. Clapping her hand over her mouth, she scuttled through to her room and closed the door firmly, sinking down into the first chair. He was working on her, was he? All that talk about finding her attractive was nothing more than blarney. Maybe he thought that if they became friends she would willingly hand the house over to him. Thank goodness she hadn't made a fool of herself, hadn't let him see that he even remotely affected her. She hadn't felt comfortable about eavesdropping, but now she was glad that she had. She would certainly be on her guard now.

CHAPTER FOUR

WHY don't plans ever work out? wondered Briony, trying yet again to start her car. Her Metro had been temperamental for a few weeks now and any second she expected Nicholas Grant to come out and offer assistance. He did not let her down. Footsteps sounded and her car door was jerked open, his head pushed inside. 'Having trouble?'

What does it look like? she felt tempted to answer, but instead she swallowed her sharp words and nodded instead. 'It won't start.'

'Release your hood; I'll take a look.'

Briony obeyed and sat silently fuming. She did not want his help; she did not want anything from him. She just wanted him out of her life altogether.

After a few minutes' fiddling he lifted his head. 'Try it now.' But again there was nothing, no response from the engine at all. 'I think it might be your alternator,' he said. 'And your plugs definitely need changing. When was the last time you had a service?'

Briony shrugged. 'Not since I bought it.'

'With winter on its way you really should get it checked over.' He came round to the side of the car again, leaning his arms on the open window and filling the space with his head and shoulders.

'I know,' answered Briony tightly, 'but having a service is low on my list of priorities at the moment.'

'Meaning you can't afford it?'

She nodded, not liking to admit that she was penniless, even though he knew it anyway. His face was far too close to hers, triggering off again those unwanted responses; she could feel her stomach curling into knots and the sudden hurried acceleration of her pulses. It was crazy and ridiculous and out of all proportion to her real feelings. It was the first time she had ever felt such a strong physical attraction to a man, and for it to be this man of all people made it a thousand times worse.

'What would you do if you broke down in some out-of-the-way place?' His face inched even closer.

'It's never happened yet,' she said with a faint shrug.

'But it might. If you like I could service your car for you, provided my father's tools are still somewhere around.'

'Can you do that?' she asked in surprise.

'Would I offer if I couldn't?' he returned drily. 'Let's take a look.'

Briony reluctantly helped him search the corners and shelves of the old stables that had been converted into a three-car garage. 'I haven't touched anything in here,' she said, 'but I haven't seen anything either. James always had his cars done at Hunters. I wasn't aware that he was a do-it-yourself man.'

'He used to be at one time,' Nicholas informed her. 'I think I took after him in that respect—I can turn my hand to most things. Ah, here we are.' He lifted up a rusty metal toolbox and set it down by her car before shooting a glance at his wristwatch. 'I might just have time to get what I need from the garage. Can I drop you off somewhere?'

Briony hesitated. She did not want to be shut in his car with him, for no matter how short a period, but neither did she want to stay at home for the rest of the day. 'You can take me to the bus-stop, if you like.'

'Where are you going?'

'To visit a friend.'

'Where does she live—or is it a he?'

'A girlfriend,' she said, adding quickly, 'and it's miles out of your way; I couldn't ask you to take me there.'

'You're not asking—I'm offering—but it strikes me that you needn't go out at all. You're only doing it because of me, aren't you?' He looked at her intently as he spoke.

Briony held his gaze. 'Not at all,' she lied. 'Rhoda and I visit each other frequently on a Saturday afternoon. We've been friends ever since our schooldays.'

'Then if you really want to go I'll take you. I'll just fetch my keys and tell Jojo where I'm going.'

In less time than she had to think about it he was out again and Briony duly clambered into the black Ferrari which he had left standing at the front of the house. It was impossible to breathe without feeling the full impact of his sensuality. Even the musky male scent of him was more intense inside the car, infiltrating her nostrils, stimulating and arousing, and she knew it was going to be the most difficult journey she had ever undertaken. She ought to have refused, ought to have insisted on using the bus, at the very least given Rhoda another ring and asked her to come here. Except that it was to get away from Nicholas Grant that she had decided to go out! Everything was conspiring against her.

Rhoda lived a twenty-minute drive from Thornton Hall and Briony knew it was going to be the longest twenty minutes of her life. She racked her brains for something to talk about, something that would take her mind off his physical presence, but all she could think of was the excitement that raced through her veins. She had to consciously remind herself that he was out to take Thornton Hall from beneath her feet, and only by doing that was she able to ignore her feelings and whip up any sort of resentment.

'Do you look like your mother?' he asked softly. 'Did she have that same wonderful hair?' He glanced across at her as he spoke and Briony got the impression that if he hadn't been driving he would have reached out and touched it. She wore it loose today, hanging over her shoulders like spun silk.

'Not quite as pale as mine,' she replied, 'but she was a blonde, yes, and we were very similar in looks. She was a very attractive woman for her age.'

'Like mother like daughter,' he murmured.

Briony grimaced, knowing full well now that his flattery was insincere, all part of the game he was playing. 'I have no wish to discuss my mother,' she said primly.

'It still hurts?'

She nodded.

'I am curious, though; if she was as attractive as you're suggesting, why did she wait so long before getting married again?'

Briony looked at him sharply. 'If you're suggesting that she was waiting for a rich man you're mistaken; she simply never met the right person. She was heartbroken when my father walked out on her; she loved him very much.'

'And you, how did you feel, without a father during all your impressionable years?'

'Very much the same as I imagine your daughter feels without a mother,' she returned sharply. 'Or have there been a succession of women in your life? Has she never wanted for a mother figure?'

'That remark was uncalled-for,' he rasped, 'but, to satisfy your curiosity, there has been the occasional woman, yes, though none who made a home with us. The oilfields are a man's domain.'

'And what are you going to do with your oilfield if you settle here?' she asked caustically, though God forbid he ever did.

'I've sold it,' he announced. 'I have nothing to keep me in Houston.'

'Sold it?' Briony echoed her amazement. This was something she had not expected.

'That's right,' he assured her, smiling grimly at the expression on her face.

'And now you're planning to buy back your father's business?'

'In due course, but I'm in no hurry; there are other more important things to do.'

'Like getting your hands on Thornton Hall,' she answered bitterly.

'Like claiming my rightful inheritance,' he amended. 'I'm sorry you're distressed about all this, Briony, but the house means a lot to me and I intend staking my claim even if the new will doesn't turn up. However, there's no reason why we shouldn't live together quite amicably. I have no plan to throw you out into the street.'

'That's very big of you,' she jeered, 'but I think you're forgetting that I'm no meek and docile girl. I intend fighting *you* every inch of the way. As far as I'm concerned Thornton Hall is *mine*, and it's staying that way, and I'm afraid I don't feel as generous—I have no intention of making you welcome; I want you out—forever!'

She was being grossly unfair, she knew that, when he had been born and brought up at the Hall for the first eighteen years of his life. Strictly speaking, it should belong to him, but he had given it all up, he had never once made the effort to come and see his father, and that was it as far as she was concerned. He was a heartless, unthinking brute, and she would fight tooth and nail to keep the house from him.

His lips quirked. 'Has anyone ever told you that you're beautiful when you're angry?'

Briony flashed him a look of contempt. 'Flattery will get you nowhere.'

'I'm speaking the truth; you're a very lovely young lady, and if you were mine I'd never leave you alone like your man does.'

'Let's leave Paul out of this,' she spat.

He lifted his broad shoulders indifferently. 'I wouldn't complain if he never turned up because then I'd have you all to myself.'

'And what is that supposed to mean?' she asked with a sharp frown.

'It means, honey, that I want to get to know you better, I want us to become friends. As I said before, I find you very attractive; I'd like to think that something deeper might develop.'

'So that I'd stop fighting you over the house?' she flashed, trying to ignore the warmth of his smile. 'Don't think you can pull the wool over my eyes; I know exactly what you're up to, and it's not going to work. I despise you, Mr Grant, I'm not in the least attracted to you, and the sooner you accept that the better.'

Again he did not look perturbed. 'Something tells me you're not speaking the truth, and if I weren't driving at this moment I'd be very tempted to prove it.'

Briony gasped at his audacity.

'As it stands, I'll save the pleasure for another occasion. Let me just say that I find your mouth infinitely kissable and I shall look forward immensely to the experience.'

What a nerve he had, this man who was nothing like his father. 'You'll wait a long time,' she spat. 'Turn left here and then left again at the end. It's the big white house on the right; you can't miss it.' She was thankful their journey was coming to an end.

'You obviously don't know me very well yet,' he grinned, turning where she had indicated. 'When I make up my mind to do something it's nearly always done straight away. I think you should bear that in mind.'

'Your threat doesn't scare me,' she answered coldly, 'and I can't imagine anything worse than kissing someone who is uncooperative. You'll be very disappointed. This is it; thank you for bringing me.' The second he stopped she scrambled out and walked towards the house without once glancing back. She was actually quivering with anger, or was it anticipation? She knew exactly what would happen if he kissed her: every single one of her emotions would surge into life. Only to him would she deny that she found him attractive.

Rhoda was married, but her husband owned a hardware store and consequently always worked on a Saturday, so it worked out very well when they wanted to spend time together. A ravishing redhead, she welcomed Briony warmly. 'Who on earth was that dishy man who dropped you off?' she asked at once.

'Don't ask,' said Briony bitterly, but when Rhoda became insistent, 'It's James's son, turned up out of the blue to lay claim to the house.'

'Can he do that?' asked Rhoda, her surprise showing in her wide blue eyes.

Briony shrugged. 'I'm not sure yet; he claims there's another will, though no one's ever seen it. Whatever, I intend fighting him every inch of the way. Can you believe he hasn't been home in eighteen years and then thinks he can take over just like that? He really is a swine and I loathe him.'

'So how come he gave you a lift if you hate him that much?'

'My car wouldn't start.'

Rhoda looked at her friend closely. 'You're telling me he's actually living at Thornton Hall with you?' And when Briony nodded, 'Goodness me, how exciting. From what I saw of him he's a real man. You never know, Briony, you might fall in love with him; that would solve all your problems.'

'And pigs might fly,' snorted Briony indelicately. 'I'm in love with Paul, in case you'd forgotten, and there's not only Nicholas to contend with, there's his insufferable daughter as well.'

'He's married?' Rhoda's face was a picture of disappointment.

Briony laughed. 'No—oh, it's a long story, but the fact is he's single and available and in other circumstances I might have fancied him, but as it is I hate his guts. Let's talk about something else.'

They tried, but somehow the conversation kept returning to Nicholas Grant, and by teatime Briony felt that no purpose had been served by coming here. 'I think I might go to the cinema,' she said as she got ready to leave.

'Can't face the thought of spending the evening with your new friend?' taunted Rhoda. 'What a pity—he could be just what you need.'

'What do you mean?' asked Briony with a frown.

'Well, I know I shouldn't be saying this, but you've been going out with Paul for so long that the relationship's gone stale. Tell me to mind my own business if it's not true, but—— '

'It is true.' Briony reluctantly made the confession. 'Though I didn't realise it until——'

'Nicholas Grant turned up?' Rhoda finished for her.

Briony nodded self-consciously.

'So there is hope?'

'No!' she said loudly. 'I hate him. Wouldn't you hate a man who was trying to turn you out of your house.'

'But you said he was quite prepared to let you go on living there even if it did prove to be his.'

'At what cost?' scoffed Briony. 'No, thank you. I don't want anything to do with him.'

Briony saw nothing of the film, even though it was one she had wanted to see for a long time. She simply could not get Nicholas out of her mind. Even his face became superimposed over the principal actor's, and in a very tender love scene she found herself filled with excitement, imagining it was herself kissing Nicholas.

So intense were her feelings that it was several minutes before she became aware what was happening, and then she looked around guiltily, convinced everyone had been watching the expressions on her face. Of course they hadn't, and she was able to relax back into her seat, but, if imagination could do that, what would the real thing do? Thank goodness there was no chance of it ever happening. Nicholas Grant was the last person she would fall in love with.

It was after eleven when she finally got home and she had planned on going straight up to bed until she saw a light on in James's study. She frowned and pushed open the door.

'Ah, come in, I was wondering what time you'd get back.' Nicholas sat in his father's swivel armchair, feet up on the desk beside an open file, a sheaf of papers in his hand, a broad, welcoming smile on his face.

'What do you think you're doing?' asked Briony sharply. She ought to have known that once she was out of the house he would waste no time in looking for James's will.

'I'm trying to find out why my father's company crashed as it did,' he answered, much to her surprise. 'Goodness me, it was founded by his own grandfather; it was as stable as any business could be.'

She flashed him a look of scorn. 'How would you have any idea how stable the company was? I worked for him, don't forget. The orders just weren't coming in. He was very worried, though I must confess I didn't realise things were as bad as they were until he told me he was selling out.'

Nicholas's eyes narrowed. 'And did the orders stop coming in all of a sudden, or was it a gradual thing, creeping up on him unawares?'

Briony thought for a moment. 'Gradual, I suppose.'

'Exactly. I think there's much more to this than anyone knows.' He got up from his seat and tipped the remains of the bottle of Glenfiddich into his glass. 'Would you care to join me in a night-cap?'

'No, thanks,' Briony replied tautly, thinking it hadn't taken him long to finish off his father's whisky.

'Did you have a pleasant day?'

'Yes, I did.' Briony stepped back a pace as he stood much closer to her than was necessary, recalling his earlier threat, but also recalling with vivid clarity the love scene in the film which she had lived every moment of with this man. Her heart raced at the memory and she went warm all over.

'Did your friend bring you home?'

Briony shook her head. 'She took me into town; I've been to the cinema.'

Nicholas frowned. 'By yourself? Did you get a taxi back?'

'No, I came on the bus.'

He swore beneath his breath. 'Why didn't you give me a ring? I had no idea that's what you were planning; I'd have come to the cinema with you. I don't like the idea of you being out by yourself so late; it's quite a walk from the bus-stop.'

Briony had no intention of admitting that she hadn't liked it either, but taxis cost money, money she was not prepared to pay when there was a convenient bus. 'Thank you for your concern, but I'm home safe, as you can see, and now I'm going to bed; I'm very tired. Goodnight, Nicholas.'

Nicholas, however, was not prepared to let her go. He moved towards the door and blocked her exit, and when she tried to push past him he pulled her into his arms.

Briony instantly began to fight. 'Let me go, you brute.'

'I've wanted to hold you like this right from the first moment I met you,' he muttered, heedless of her struggles. 'You're enough to drive a man insane, do you know that? And I especially love your hair.' He lifted it either side of her face, twisting it through his fingers, imprisoning her in an entirely different way.

'You're drunk!' she cried. 'Let go of me this instant.'

'I never get drunk,' he assured her. 'It's a sign of weakness. I know exactly what I'm doing, Briony. I've sat here tonight waiting for you, waiting for this moment.' His face swooped down towards hers, his grip on her hair tightening so that she was unable to move without hurting herself, and when his lips met hers excitement beyond reason raced through her veins. Every sense clamoured into instant response, every sensual thought she had ever had crowded in on her.

It was happening as she had known it would happen, but, whatever she felt, she had no intention of letting him see it. She knew exactly what game he was playing and there was definitely only going to be one winner, and that was her. Emotional blackmail was something she would not give way to.

The kiss lasted no more than a few seconds, a few spine-tingling seconds, amazing her in its intensity, and yet even though her outward response had been negative he still smiled, still seemed satisfied. She wondered if it was possible that he had guessed how she felt, guessed that she'd had to make an effort to hide her feelings. Could he be that perceptive? She sincerely hoped not.

'A most pleasant experience,' he announced, leaning back against the door, a smile of pure satisfaction on his face. 'Definitely an exercise I'd like to repeat.'

Briony eyed him coldly, trying to still the irritating trembling in her veins. 'If you think you can get through to me that way you're mistaken; you're simply lowering my opinion of you.' She made her words harsh and condemning and had the satisfaction of seeing his jaw go tense. 'As far as I'm concerned, using your sex appeal is about as low as you can get. Goodnight, Nicholas.'

She felt his eyes on her as she marched along the hall, her chin high, her back straight, and not until she had turned the corner to go up the stairs did she relax and let out a sigh of sheer relief. She even paused a moment to gather her senses. His kiss had been all and more than she had expected, confirming beyond any shadow of doubt how strong her physical attraction to him was. It was such an unreal situation that she could not believe it was happening. A strange man came and declared the house was rightfully his and instead of hating him she found herself sexually attracted to him! It did not make sense. She must fight it with all of her might.

She did not hear Nicholas leave the study; she did not hear him walk along the corridor; she was not aware of his presence until he came up suddenly behind her. 'What's this?' His tone was faintly derogative. 'Something on your mind, Briony?'

He knew! Damn the man—he knew. She looked at him coldly and haughtily. 'Whatever gave you that impression? I was just—just admiring this painting. It was one of James's favourites.'

He looked first at the Constable reproduction and then at her. 'Is that so? I always thought Rubens was his favourite artist.'

'Maybe a man's tastes change,' she said vaguely.

'And maybe you're making it up because you don't want me to know the real reason you're standing here.' He reached out and touched her cheek with a gentle finger. 'There's no need to be ashamed because you feel some sort of response. It's a perfectly natural thing to happen.'

'Ashamed? Responsive?' she echoed unsteadily, wanting to back away from him but knowing that any counter movement would confirm, in his opinion anyway, that she was all too aware of his sensuality. 'You're imagining things; you're seeing what you want to see, and I'm afraid you're very wrong.'

'You love darling Paul too much to be attracted to another man, is that what you're trying to say?' His lips twisted into a sceptical smile and his fingertips continued to stroke her skin. 'Or is it that you're feeling guilty? You wish it wasn't happening to you but you can't help it?'

'You're insane,' she snapped. 'I don't feel anything.'

His black eyes looked amusedly into hers and deliberately his fingers moved to touch the corners of her mouth, tracing its fullness, pulling down her bottom lip and brushing the soft moistness inside, finally lowering his head to kiss the same spot very gently.

Briony felt herself melting on the spot and it was all she could do to maintain indifference; in fact it was the hardest thing she had ever had to do in her life. But somehow she managed it and when he finally lifted his head she glared at him furiously. 'Does that satisfy you?'

'I don't know about satisfaction,' he said with wry humour, 'but it certainly tells me a lot about your will-power. I think I'm going to have to break it down.'

Shaking her head furiously, Briony swung away from him and headed up the stairs. 'You're insane, you're out of your mind. All you're doing is making me hate you even more.'

'Now that is a pity, because it wasn't my intention at all.'

'Then why force yourself on me when you know how I feel?' she flung, pausing a moment to glare back at him.

'Oh, yes, I know how you feel all right,' he agreed smilingly, 'and it's a whole lot different from what you say. The truth of the matter is, Briony, that you're as attracted to me as I am to you. Why don't you admit it?'

'How dare you?' she cried. 'How dare you make such assumptions? You know nothing. You're the last man on earth I'd ever feel anything for. Touch me again and I'll make jolly sure you regret it.'

After one final glare in his direction she continued up the stairs and safely reached the privacy of her room. One day, less than one day he had been here, and already she felt a nervous wreck.

CHAPTER FIVE

BRIONY was awoken the next morning by a loud female voice echoing along the corridors of the house. For an instant she could not think what was happening, so used was she to complete silence, and then it came back to her that Nicholas and his daughter had landed themselves on her and it was this girl who was making so much noise.

She pulled the sheets over her head but it made no difference. She was wide awake and might as well get up even though a glance at the clock showed her it was only seven o'clock.

When she finally went downstairs Josephine was in the kitchen eating toast, and the work surface where she had buttered and cut the toast was black and sticky with burnt breadcrumbs. 'Good morning, Josephine.' Briony bit back a swift reprimand, greeting her pleasantly instead.

'Don't call me Josephine, I don't like it,' was all the response she got. 'Everyone calls me Jo.'

Except her father, thought Briony, but she infinitely preferred Jo to Jojo and she smiled. 'Very well, Jo it shall be. Did you sleep well?'

'No, I didn't,' snapped the girl. 'I hate this house; I hate England; I want to go home.'

'Your father thought he was doing the right thing.'

'It's all right for him—he used to live here, he likes it here, he was always talking about it, telling me what a wonderful place it was and that he wanted to bring me here one day. He was sure I would like it as well, he said, but he was wrong; I don't, and I don't want to stay.'

'What sort of a house did you have in Houston?'

'We only had an apartment, but it was fabulous and we had views over the river, and the city centre is fantastic, almost like New York. That's where I'd really like to live. Nicholas took me there once.'

'Have you seen much of England?' asked Briony. 'You can't judge the whole country by one small part.'

'I don't want to see it,' complained Josephine. 'I never wanted to come in the first place.' And, so saying, she bounced out of the room.

'Just a minute, Jo,' Briony called after her.

The girl turned and looked back, a petulant expression on her pretty face.

'The agreement is that you leave the kitchen as you find it.'

'I'm not doing housework,' she replied with a toss of her head.

'And nor am I going to clean up after you,' returned Briony sharply.

At that moment Nicholas joined his daughter in the doorway. Freshly showered, black hair curling crisply, a white shirt contrasting strongly with his tanned skin, he was the epitome of a healthy male animal. 'What's going on here?'

Briony shook off the feelings that began to assail her and pointed to the work surface. 'Jo made that mess; I think she should clean it up.'

'I think she should too,' said Nicholas. 'Jojo?'

With a great deal of sighing and black looks in Briony's direction, the girl did as she was told, rinsing the dishcloth afterwards and putting it back where she had found it. 'May I go now?'

'You may,' agreed Nicholas, 'but just remember another time to tidy up after you.' When she had gone he gave Briony an apologetic smile. 'I'm sorry about that; it shouldn't happen again.'

'Has she always been a difficult child?' she rasped.

He frowned at her harsh words. 'Jojo's not difficult; she's just at that age when she resents being told what to do.'

'She resents being here, full stop,' said Briony sharply.

He nodded. 'But she'll get used to it. Once she starts college and makes friends it will make all the difference.'

Briony hoped so. 'I'd also appreciate it if you'd stop her shouting at the top of her voice so early in the morning. I usually have a lie-in on a Sunday.'

'Jo and I have always been early risers,' he grinned unrepentantly, 'and we've always yelled to each other from room to room.'

'That was when you didn't have to think of anyone else,' Briony reproved.

'It strikes me that the rules here are going to be endless.' He frowned as suddenly as he had smiled. 'It also strikes me that they're all on your side. Haven't you stopped to think that it might be as difficult for us as it is for you?'

'It was your choice to live here,' Briony reminded him.

'But not my choice that a strange woman should claim possession of my father's house. Have you any idea how hard that discovery was for me to swallow? For your information, I don't particularly like the situation either, but it's a matter of making the best of it for the time being.'

'Oh, no,' said Briony, vigorously shaking her head. 'It's not a matter of making the best of it at all. It's sheer perverseness that made you insist on moving in. You didn't like to see *me* here, that's the trouble. You came expecting to find the house sitting empty waiting for you and then found it belonged to me. That's what's really bothering you, isn't it?' She was furious now, actually shaking.

Last night she had lain in bed and thought about nothing but the kiss he had given her, the kiss which had sparked into life new and wondrous feelings, emotions which had never revealed themselves in Paul's company. At this moment she could cheerfully have murdered him.

'I'm sure that if the positions were reversed you would feel the same,' he answered tersely.

Briony drew in her breath swiftly and savagely. 'If James knew you were trying to get rid of me he'd turn over in his grave.'

'Have I said that I want you out?' His tone was cold and distant, his face taut and aggressive, and, without waiting for her to answer, he snapped, 'No, I haven't, and you know it.'

'How about when I get married?' she challenged, her smoky eyes equally cold on his. 'Are we still all going to live here as one big, happy family?'

'You're going to marry this wimp?' he asked, his chin tilted all of a sudden, black eyes disbelieving.

'One day, yes,' she replied defensively, even though the thought now of marrying Paul was a much less attractive proposition than it had been before Nicholas turned up.

'One day!' he tossed, his tone scornful. 'A six-year courtship and no sign of even an engagement. I think you're living in a dream world. This guy's playing you along and it's time you realised it.'

Furiously Briony glared at him. 'You have no right running Paul down when you don't even known him.'

'I've heard enough to form an opinion,' said Nicholas, crossing the room and picking up the kettle, checking there was enough water in before switching it on. 'Can I make you a drink while I'm doing mine?' His voice was so casual and friendly that it was difficult to believe they had just been at each other's throats.

Knowing it would be ungracious to refuse, Briony nodded. 'Tea, please, very weak, no milk or sugar.'

'What are you going to have to eat?'

'Cornflakes.'

His brows rose. 'No bacon and egg, the good old traditional English breakfast? I bought some bacon yesterday; we can share if you like?'

'No, thanks,' she said. 'Cereal's fine.' And she proceeded to reach the packet out of the cupboard. With a bit of luck she would have finished before his breakfast was cooked. The prospect of eating together was abhorrent.

'What time are your viewers due?'

Briony frowned faintly and then her face cleared. In all the fuss over Josephine she had forgotten that someone was coming to look at the house. 'Ten o'clock.'

'So we have plenty of time. Do you like your milk hot or cold?' He reached the bottle out of the fridge and paused with it in his hand.

'Cold, thank you,' replied Briony, taking it from him. He was being so polite and helpful it was unreal, and she hoped there weren't going to be many mornings when they shared the kitchen like this.

'I actually think you should ring and tell them that the Hall's no longer for sale.'

'Don't start that again,' snapped Briony, pausing in the act of pouring milk over her cornflakes. 'As far as I'm concerned it still is, unless of course you've already found the other will?'

'You know damn well I haven't,' he growled, his mouth tightening. 'And not until every stone has been turned will I let you sell. I shall stop you every inch of the way.'

Briony shrugged and continued to eat her breakfast and as soon as she had finished she popped her dish and mug into the dishwasher and left the kitchen. To her surprise Nicholas let her go.

The Morgans arrived at five minutes to the hour and, to Briony's annoyance, when the doorbell rang Nicholas met her in the hallway to answer it, and when she opened the door he was the first one to hold out his hand. 'How do you do? Nicholas Grant Thornton's the name; do come in and let me show you around.' All trace of his American accent had gone; he was very much the British squire.

Briony fumed, but good manners prevented her from speaking her mind. 'And I'm Briony Weston,' she said firmly, 'the present owner of Thornton Hall.'

The couple entered and Mr Morgan frowned faintly, looking from one to the other. 'You say your name's Thornton?' he addressed Nicholas. 'One of *the* Thorntons?'

'The very last one,' came the smiling response.

The man shook his head. 'I understood that Miss Weston lived here alone and that was why she wanted to sell.'

'That's right,' put in Briony firmly. 'I——'

'That *was* the case,' cut in Nicholas. 'I've only just come back after living in America for many years. Miss Weston was unaware of my existence.'

'Are you saying,' frowned the older man, 'that the house is no longer on the market?'

'He's not saying that at all,' said Briony quickly. 'The house still belongs to me and I have every intention of selling.'

Nicholas spoke up again. 'Actually that might not be strictly true. We've been talking, Miss Weston and I, only this morning, as a matter of fact, and we've reached a compromise. It actually might not be necessary to sell.'

Briony gasped, the Morgans looked surprised, and Nicholas continued to smile.

'What Mr Grant—er—Thornton is trying to say,' said Briony, 'is that there's some slight controversy over ownership. He seems to think that it belongs to him, and I say it's mine, and until it's sorted it can't actually be sold. Nevertheless you're still welcome to look around and once everything's been resolved then I'll get in touch with you again.'

Mr Morgan shook his head, frowning harshly. 'It looks to me as though we're wasting our time. You could have had the decency to phone and explain and save us a journey. Come along, Elizabeth.' His wife looked put out too as they turned to leave.

'You have my sincere apologies,' said Nicholas, 'but as I've only just returned there really hasn't been very much time to discuss our plans for the house. It's not Miss Weston's fault, it's mine entirely; I am most sorry.'

When they had left Briony rounded on him angrily. 'You had no right talking like that. This isn't your house yet, and if I have anything to do with it it never will be.'

'What beautiful eyes you have.' He gave a satisfied smile. 'It's worth getting you angry to see how they flash. But there's no doubt in my mind that the house *will* be mine one day—one day soon, I hope—so it's as well the Morgans were sent on their way.'

'It will never be yours.' Red-hot fury scorched her cheeks and ran like molten metal through her veins. 'There is no will; I'd definitely have found it if there were.'

'You saw my father's letter.'

'Which you could have easily written yourself.'

'Is that what you think?' A muscle suddenly jerked in his jaw.

'I wouldn't put anything past you,' she snapped. 'For all I know you might not even be James's son; it could all be some huge con trick so that you can get your hands on the house.' She was speaking irrationally and knew it, but he made her so mad. 'As a matter of fact,' she added fiercely, 'I want you out now, both of you. I don't care what the solicitor said; this is *my* house and if I don't want you here then I don't have to put up with you.'

'Briony, calm down.' Nicholas put his hands on her shoulders. 'You're over-reacting.'

'Over-reacting?' she yelled, twisting swiftly away from him. 'How can you possibly say that after you've just behaved as though Thornton Hall is already yours?'

'It's what my father wanted,' he explained patiently.

'And I have only your word for that,' she spat back. 'The way I look at it, you're living in a dream world. The very fact that he denied your existence all these years proves he wanted nothing more to do with you. I don't believe he wrote that letter.'

'Then feel free to have it examined by a graphologist,' he retorted. He stood in front of her, thumbs hooked into the pockets of his trousers, tall, threatening, determined. Although a faint smile played about his lips the rest of his face was hard, eyes coldly piercing. A determined opponent.

Briony jutted her chin and returned his gaze coldly. 'I might even do that, but I'll wait until Richard Brent returns. He's the only one who can vouch for your identity, although I doubt that even he, after all this time, can vouch for your integrity, and that is, after all, what counts.'

'What a fiery creature you are.' Before Briony could anticipate his actions his arms shot around her and she was pulled hard against his powerfully muscled body.

The familiar gamut of emotions catapulted into life and it nauseated her that she could feel such a response in the midst of her anger. 'Let me go!' she yelled, but he merely laughed harshly and tightened his embrace.

'It might be interesting to find out whether you're as passionate in other ways.'

'If you don't release me I'll scream the place down,' she threatened.

'And who's to hear, except my daughter?'

'Isn't that enough? What would she think if she saw you molesting me?'

'That's rather a harsh word, Briony.' A firm finger brought her chin up so that their eyes met, and she saw the flash of anger.

'So you tell me what you're doing?' she spat, struggling ineffectively, hating him and yet feeling an exciting clamour of her senses at the same time.

'I'm holding a beautiful young woman in my arms. I'm not about to rape her or anything like that. In fact I plan on doing nothing that she doesn't want herself.'

Oh, God, he knew! He was aware of every sensation that ran through her. She felt utterly degraded and increased her struggles, but still to no effect. In fact he seemed to be enjoying the contest and she knew he would not let her go until he had accomplished whatever it was he planned to do.

Perhaps she ought not to struggle, perhaps she ought to lie passive in his arms, but what would happen then? Would he kiss her, caress her? Briony felt confusion such as she had never felt before. 'This is insanity,' she cried. 'You're a maniac and I demand that you let me go this instant.'

'You're so very beautiful when you're angry.' He ignored her pleas altogether. 'And do you know you feel just right in my arms?' A hand slid up to her nape and began stroking, slowly and seductively.

'This is insanity,' she hissed.

'Has Paul never done this to you?' The low growl of his voice sent a further shiver down her spine. 'Or this?' He lowered his head and nuzzled the soft skin behind her ear. 'Or this?' he added, taking her lobe between his fine white teeth and nipping gently.

'Let's leave Paul out of this,' she spat, feeling her whole body convulse with pleasure.

'Why should we when it's his girl I'm holding? Do you think he'd mind? Would he be very angry? Or doesn't he love you enough to care?'

Briony tried to wrest her head away, but his hand held her in a vice-like grip. 'Of course he cares,' she shot back. 'You'll soon find out when I tell him what you've been doing.'

'You'd do that?' He looked surprised.

'Naturally, and he'll make jolly sure that you don't lay your hands on me again.' She was not certain that she would tell Paul, but there was no harm in letting Nicholas sweat.

'And when will he be back, this macho man of yours?' He assaulted her other ear this time, tongue and teeth probing, tasting, arousing.

'Any day now.' She tried to squirm away.

'But you're not exactly sure when?' His head came up and he looked at her in sudden surprise. 'Doesn't he keep you up to date with his movements?'

'Of course he does,' she replied defensively. Except that on this occasion she hadn't heard from him since he left. It was unusual for him not to telephone and as he hadn't given her the name of his hotel all she could do was wait until he did turn up. She hoped it wouldn't be too long.

'It doesn't leave me much time to work on you.'

Briony's eyes widened. 'What do you mean, "work on me"?'

'Oh, come on,' he returned, 'you're surely not as naïve as all that?'

'If you mean what I think you mean,' she snapped, 'you can forget it. I'm not interested in you in any way, shape or form. My skin crawls at your touch and I demand that you let me go this instant.'

A disbelieving smile curved the fullness of his lips. 'Your skin crawls, does it? Now that *is* interesting, because my in-built sense detector tells me that it's reacting in a very different way. In actual fact I can feel the warmth of your body, the tiny prickles of awareness that are running through your veins; even your heartbeat I can feel, and it's anything but regular. I think, Miss Briony Weston, that you're telling me lies.'

'I don't care what you think,' she snapped, horrified that he was so close to the truth. 'I don't want you near me. If I have to put up with you in the house then so be it, but I intend to make very certain that there's a distance kept between us. Now let me go.' She wriggled furiously, but still he retained his hold on her.

'This I like,' he said with a smile. 'It's not often you find a girl as prepared to do battle as you. It's very exciting.'

'You mean you're not used to girls resisting you?' she derided. 'Is that why you're persevering? Is it bad for your ego to find someone who doesn't instantly respond?'

'My ego has nothing to do with it,' he told her firmly, 'and if you were truthful you'd admit that your body responds to mine.'

'You're a big-headed bas——'

'Now, now, Briony,' he stopped her. 'Such unladylike language is bad for your image. How can you have the face of an angel and think such harsh thoughts?'

'Only where you're concerned,' she snapped, and finally, thankfully, she managed to wrench herself free.

She felt her heart throbbing in her breast and she wanted to run up the stairs to the comparative safety of her room. Only pride made her walk away with slow dignity.

'What are you going to do with yourself today?'

Nicholas's unexpected question halted her in her tracks, but she did not look around. 'I think that's my business,' she said over her shoulder. Normally she had Paul to keep her company. Today she had made no plans at all, was going to perhaps potter around in the garden, do a few odd jobs—that was until Nicholas and his daughter had turned up on the scene. Now she wanted to steer clear of him and that would be virtually impossible if she stayed in the house.

She turned, finally. 'How about you?'

'I thought I might take Jojo out; she's not seen much of the Staffordshire countryside. Would you like to come with us?' He must have known she would refuse, yet he still managed to look vaguely disappointed when she shook her head. 'In case you do plan to go out I've fixed your car.'

Grudgingly, Briony thanked him. 'I didn't expect you to service it so quickly. I'm very grateful. I was wondering how I'd get to work tomorrow.'

'The pleasure's all mine,' he told her with a quirky smile. 'Besides, it's good to keep one's hand in. But in case you do go somewhere, perhaps I ought to have a key? I should hate to find myself locked out.' There was a sudden steely glint in his eye as he spoke.

'I'll be here,' returned Briony caustically.

'I still think it would be for the best. You never know— we might be late, very late; you could have gone to bed. I should hate to disturb you.'

The cynicism in his voice did not escape her, but he was right: she wouldn't take kindly to being knocked up out of her bed, though she did not believe for one moment he would be that late. However there would be other occasions too, like when she was at work; it would be petty to refuse him a key. She gave a tiny shrug. 'Very well, if you insist; there's one on the hook behind the kitchen door.' She continued on her way up the stairs.

About half an hour went by before she heard her two unwanted guests leave. During all that time Briony had sat in a chair at her bedroom window, a magazine in her lap, but her eyes on Nicholas's car in the drive. Even seeing him walk across to it, his black leather jacket flung casually over his shoulders, made her pulses accelerate, and she felt cross with herself for being so weak.

How could it happen? How could she feel such a strong physical attraction to a man who was her worst enemy? Why had she let it happen? There was no answer to any of her questions.

Although there was work to be done in the house and garden—plenty of it—she instead made her way down to James's study. She was confident that Nicholas had already made a thorough search for the missing will, but knew that she wouldn't rest until she had looked herself. The thing was, where to begin? His safe was the obvious place, but she had been through that many times.

The file Nicholas had been looking at was still on the desk and she picked it up curiously. They were copies of the company accounts, and it confirmed her statement that during the last five years of trading it had been slowly going downhill until James had had no option but to sell. It was odd, considering that the firm had been going well for over a hundred years, and she could not think why his customers had started placing their orders elsewhere.

But it wasn't this she was here to puzzle over this morning, it was James's latest will, or rather the lack of it, and if it wasn't in his safe or filing-cabinet—that too had been gone through after his death—it only left the bookshelves. Had he slipped it inside a book by mistake?

Or perhaps deliberately? And if he had, which book? There were hundreds of them. It would be like looking for the proverbial needle in a haystack.

There were books on all manner of subjects, ranging from world affairs to a history of their own tiny village, from gardening to photography to golf to—wait a minute, she thought—a history of Tissingdale. Her eyes went back to the slim blue volume tucked tightly between other books. Even if it didn't yield the will it might tell her something about the feud between the Thorntons and the Camerons.

Indeed it did. As far back as the fourteenth century a certain William Thornton had charged the Camerons with breaking into his park and taking twenty deer, and all sorts of things happened after that including the Camerons taking over the Thorntons' manor house when there were no more male heirs.

In the eighteenth century Thomas Thornton—a descendant of one of the daughters who had reverted to his family name—challenged the Camerons and eventually ousted them from the manor. He bred three sons and when one of them fell in love with a Cameron girl the feuding began all over again. The son got killed. And this son was one of James's great-uncles. She could understand now James's animosity towards the Camerons.

Briony put the book down and stretched. She'd sat here for two hours entirely engrossed, forgetting her original purpose. It was fascinating reading and she was surprised that Nicholas hadn't known the furore he would cause by going out with a member of the infamous Cameron family. And at what cost to himself? None of it had worked out; his father had died without him speaking to him again. That was the greatest pity of all.

CHAPTER SIX

NICHOLAS and Josephine returned much earlier than Briony expected. She had cooked a chicken for her lunch and returned to James's study to make a further search for the will. She heard the front door open and close, heard Jo bound up the stairs, listened for Nicholas's movements, and was totally surprised when he came straight into the study.

'Just as I thought,' he said sharply.

'What do you mean?' Briony straightened from her perusal of the lower shelves and felt a surge of her senses at the mere sight of him. Even the fact that his angular face was harsh with accusation, even the fact that they could never be friends, only enemies, made no difference to the way he affected her.

His black eyes searched into hers. 'You're looking for my father's will, aren't you?'

'So what if I am?' challenged Briony. Her eyes were defensive, her chin jutting, her whole body rejecting him, belying the feelings that were traitorously raging inside her.

'And have you found it?' he asked. There was a tautness in him too, a wariness, a readiness to accuse her of goodness knew what.

Briony resented his attitude and felt like walking out of the room—except that she knew he would restrain her if she dared leave without answering. What did he think she was going to do—burn the will if she found it? Protect her own interests? Make sure he never got his hands on the house? She eyed him stonily. 'No, I have not found it; I really have no idea where it can be.'

'Do I believe you?' he asked, his tone menacingly quiet.

Briony lifted her shoulders in an expressive shrug. 'It's up to you; I'm not in the habit of lying.'

'Maybe not normally,' he concurred, 'though I think you'll agree this is an unusual and major issue.'

'Are you suggesting that I might have found the will and destroyed it?' she asked tersely.

Their eyes met and held, his coal-black and as hard as polished jet, hers fierce and sparking. 'I think you might have that in mind,' he said, and although he spoke quietly there was nevertheless a hard note of recrimination in his voice.

'You swine!' cried Briony viciously. 'I might hate the sight of you, and hate even more the thought of your taking over this house, but I would never resort to something like that, never.'

'No?' Straggly black brows rose and it was clear he did not believe her.

'*No*!' she tossed back. 'Maybe *you* wouldn't think twice about doing something so dishonest, but I certainly would. *If* I find the will I shall give it to Richard Brent, it's as simple as that.'

'But you still have your doubts that it exists?'

'Exactly,' she retorted.

'Despite my father's letter?'

Briony gave a sigh of exasperation. 'You know what I feel about that.'

'Really, Briony, you better than anyone should know his writing.' He took a step closer to her and the powerful male muskiness of him reached her nostrils. She felt more aware of him than ever and was conscious of her heart banging violently against her rib-cage.

She tried to walk past him, but he caught her wrist in a grip of iron. 'Where are you going?' he growled.

'Isn't it clear?' she snapped. 'Away from you. I don't like the attitude you're adopting. I've never done anything underhand in all my life and I don't intend to start now. Will you please let me go?'

His mouth curled into an infuriating smile. 'Do you know, Briony, when you're angry like this, all I want to do is kiss you?' And at her sudden jerk of disbelief, 'Yes, I thought that would shock you. It's a pity you find kissing me so distasteful, because personally I rather enjoy it.'

'I guess you'd enjoy kissing anybody.' Briony stopped struggling and waited for him to release her wrist.

A harsh frown savaged his angular face. 'If I were that type of man I'd have taken advantage of you long before now. I resent that implication, Briony.'

'And I resent you forcing your way into this house. It's all most unorthodox and unacceptable.'

'Really?' A mocking brow rose.

'You know very well it is,' she retorted angrily.

'I know only that you're the most attractive woman I've met in a long time.' His smile was all-encompassing, sending a tingle through every inch of her body.

Briony shook her head in disbelief. 'And what has that to do with your laying claim to Thornton Hall? Is it the house you're interested in or me?'

He gave a short bark of laughter and at the same time the fingers on his free hand traced her spine, slowly and deliberately, sliding up beneath the heavy fall of her hair, coming to a halt when they reached her nape. 'Is there any reason why it can't be both?'

'Every reason,' she claimed breathlessly. 'Would you have still insisted on moving in if I'd been fat and ugly?'

'Without a doubt,' he replied. 'You, my dear girl, are an added bonus.'

'And one you intend making the most of, given half a chance?' she asked sourly.

'Your words, not mine.' Again a smile played about his lips and she knew he was enjoying the situation. He was playing with her as a cat played with a mouse, seeing how far he could push her, trying to assess her response. 'Look, Briony,' he said after a moment, 'you can either accept the situation and make the most of it, or live a life of misery. Either way you're stuck with me until the will is found.'

Briony shook her head in disbelief. 'Are you suggesting that you might stay *forever*?' She was still confident it did not exist, that although James had said he intended leaving the house to his son he had never actually got round to doing anything about it.

'I'm working on the theory that eventually you'll have got so used to me being here that you won't want me to go.'

Briony drew in a convulsive breath. 'You have a nerve. The truth of the matter is that I cannot wait to get rid of you—that's why I've been looking for the will—and once every corner of the house has been searched I shall take great pleasure in kicking you out.'

He stiffened as she spoke and she felt the rigidness in his body against her. 'Haven't you yet got it into your beautiful head that this house is remaining in the Thornton family, no matter what the circumstances?'

'You remind me of Thomas Thornton,' she muttered.

Nicholas frowned. 'Who the hell is he?'

'I believe he was your great-great-uncle.'

He was so surprised that he let her go. 'My great-great-uncle? I've never heard of him. How do you know so much?'

'I found a book. I actually thought the will might be tucked away inside, but it wasn't. It's a complete history of Tissingdale and all the different families—including the Camerons,' she added softly.

Nicholas frowned and looked thoughtful all of a sudden. 'There was so much my father didn't tell me. I'd never heard of a feud with the Camerons before I started going out with Leonora. And even when he demanded that I give her up he still didn't tell me everything, just that they were an undesirable family. Where is this book? I'd like to read it.'

Briony moved a few paces away from him and this time he did not try to stop her. 'It's there on the desk,' she told him, and as soon as he had walked over to it she left the study.

It was over an hour later when Nicholas came looking for her. She was in her bedroom with its four-poster bed and relaxing cream, green and pink décor. He pounded on the door. 'Briony, there's something I want to discuss with you.'

'Won't it wait?' she asked impatiently. She had actually only come up for a magazine, but his imperious attitude annoyed her.

'No, it won't wait,' he yelled back. 'Do I have to come in and fetch you?'

There was no way she wanted Nicholas in her room. She could see him already in her mind's eye—raw-boned face, dark, all-seeing eyes, a sweep of black hair that needed taming, and a tall, rangy body full of unleashed power.

Reluctantly she opened her door and followed him downstairs. Even with a back view she could still feel the full impact of his sensuality and wondered whether it was always going to be like this. She hated being a slave to her emotions.

The history book of Tissingdale was still open on the desk and he tapped it with impatient fingers. 'There are no other books, I take it? Nothing with more up-to-date information?'

Briony shook her head. 'Not that I've seen.'

'That's a pity.' Nicholas frowned from his seat once again at his father's desk. 'There really does seem to have been a raging feud between the two families, more than my father ever said, more than Leonora's father told her, although he was, in my opinion, unreasonably angry when he discovered we were going out with each other. Neither of the families have a good word to say for the other.'

'Some people are like that.' She sat down on an armchair at the other side of the room, looking at Nicholas across the expanse of carpet, hoping that distance would dull her awareness, but it didn't. Her senses were just as confused as they had been when she stood right next to him. It was an entirely unreal situation and she wished she knew how to handle it. The longer Nicholas stayed, the worse it would become—that was a fact.

'I can't understand why my father never told me the true facts. Do you know what, Briony? I think the Camerons had something to do with his business failing.'

Briony gave a short, sharp gasp. 'How can that be?'

'I'm not sure yet,' he said slowly, 'but I've sat here thinking. As you know I went through his accounts the other day and the year orders started to fall off is a very significant one.'

'In what way?'

He sat back in the chair, for a few moments deep in thought, and when he spoke it seemed to be about an entirely unrelated subject. Nevertheless Briony sat quietly and listened. 'When Jojo was little she constantly asked me about her mother. I had lots of photographs of Leonora and she used to look at them and ask when she was coming home. "One day," I kept telling her, "one day."

'When Jojo was ten years old I found her crying in her room and she said it was because she hadn't got a mother and all the other girls at school had. Up until then I'd made no attempt to get in touch with Leonora. I assumed she'd gone home and she could even have got married, but I decided "nothing ventured, nothing gained", so I tried to telephone her here in England.'

'What happened?' asked Briony, sitting forward in her seat. All these little snippets of information gave her an insight into his character. There was so much about him that she did not know.

'I spoke to her father. Apparently he hadn't seen or heard from her since the day we'd both left England; he had presumed that we were still together. When I told him it hadn't worked out he swore violently, called me all the names under the sun, and slammed the phone down. He was definitely not a happy man. And I think it was about that time that my father started experiencing difficulties.'

'You mean—you think that——'

'I most certainly do,' he interjected firmly. 'Charles Cameron was furious because his daughter hadn't come home after we split up, and he blamed me for it. As he had no idea where I lived—except that it was in America somewhere—he decided to take his vengeance out on my father.'

'You really think that's what happened?' Briony personally thought it sounded rather fanciful.

'The more I think about it the more sure I am,' he said firmly. 'I'm definitely going to delve more deeply, and woe betide that man if my suspicions are correct.'

'You mean you intend to carry on this silly feud?' she asked, shocked.

'You've got it right in one, lady. No one does the dirty on a Thornton and gets away with it. I definitely shan't rest now until the company reverts to its rightful owner.'

'Meaning you?'

He inclined his head. 'Yours truly.'

'You'll need a great deal of money to buy it off Normac. They've expanded considerably since your father's day.'

'I have the money,' he said offhandedly. 'Is that what they're trading as now, Normac?'

Briony nodded.

'And if my guess is right the directors will all be Camerons.'

'You mean you think the Camerons bought the company?'

'I'm sure of it.'

'I think you're wrong,' said Briony. 'I worked for them for a short time, don't forget, until they made me redundant. There was definitely no one of that name on the board.'

'Nevertheless, I'm damn sure there's some connection.' He pushed himself up and crossed the room. 'And first thing tomorrow I intend finding out. Meanwhile——' his smile was slow and all encompassing '—I can think of much more interesting ways to occupy myself.'

She ought to have been warned, but somehow her brain wasn't functioning properly, and when he took her hands and helped her to her feet all she could think of was that the nearness of him thrilled right through her. But when his arms slid around her and she was propelled against his hard, muscular body she knew that she had to stop him, and stop him quickly before common sense was overruled by physical need. 'What are you doing?' Her tone was sharp as she fought to free herself.

A swift spasm of annoyance darkened his face, but he did not let her go; his grip tightened instead. 'Why

is it that whenever I touch you you back off?' he growled.
'Anyone would think I had two heads.'

'What do you think?' she challenged. 'Maybe I have
no control over your using this house, but I have plenty
to say about your trying to use me.'

'I never *use* women,' he countered harshly. 'You
cannot refute that your body responds to mine. I've seen
it, felt it, am aware of it. Why deny yourself what you
know you want?'

'What I want?' she questioned disbelievingly. 'I don't
want *this*, I don't want any intimacy between us at all;
it will solve nothing. In fact it will make matters worse.'

'But you cannot deny that you do have some sort of
feelings for me?' he insisted.

'Oh, yes, I have feelings,' Briony snapped. 'Hatred
being the predominant one.'

'All in your mind,' he derided. 'You just won't admit,
even to yourself, that your feelings are in fact just the
opposite.'

Briony frowned. 'As far as I'm concerned the opposite of hatred is love—and you're the last person on
earth I'd fall in love with. Just get your hands off me,
will you?'

'Oh, no,' he said with a grim smile, 'I'm not letting
you go yet. Have you any idea what it's like living with
you, being driven crazy by the very sight of you?'

Briony looked up at him sharply. 'Don't spin me that
tale. This is all a devious plot to try and get me on your
side—just in case the will is never found. Don't think I
can't see right through you; I know exactly what your
game is.'

His lips quirked at her words. 'It could be useful, yes,
getting you on my side, but it's not something I've given
any thought to. We could have met in any circumstances
and I would have found you attractive—and I think the
same can be said for you?'

Briony closed her eyes, unable to look at him, unable to lie again.

Nicholas groaned, as if he knew exactly what she was thinking, and his arms about her tightened, and Briony found herself unable to stop his kisses, not even wanting to. It was the inevitable conclusion of what he had set out to do.

Their mouths fusing together created sensations that were out of this world, unlike anything she had ever experienced before. Paul's kisses paled into insignificance in comparison.

She could not stop herself from touching him, feeling the hardness of his body beneath the soft material of his shirt, moving timidly up his chest to his shoulders, clinging, enjoying, gasping when his mouth left hers to assault the slender, pulsating column of her throat.

As his lips moved ever lower, pushing inside the collar of her blouse to taste and explore, she felt a growing delirium. She could not stop him; she wanted him to touch her, to kiss her, to caress her.

A tiny whimper of pleasure escaped the back of her throat and her fingers curled into the thickness of his hair. He looked down at her questioningly, an intensity in his dark eyes that made her heart beat even faster, and he stroked the flushed skin of her cheek with incredibly light fingertips.

'Women are eternally unpredictable,' he said softly, his mouth caressing hers. 'One moment resisting, the next soft and pliant.'

'I'm not——' began Briony, but her protest faded even as it formed on her lips.

His arm pulled her closer as his kiss deepened and her senses beat an erotic rhythm. Heat burned through her and her fingers clenched in his black hair, holding him to her, wanting this moment to go on for ever. All sane thoughts had fled; she knew only that this man was awakening feelings of such ferocity that her whole body did not feel as though it belonged to her any more.

'Nick, are you in there? I want...' Josephine's voice tailed off as she saw the two of them embracing, her pretty face convulsing into a picture of horror and distaste.

When Josephine burst in Briony felt instant shame and would have pulled out of Nicholas's arms had he not held her with resolute tightness. 'Haven't you ever thought of knocking?' he asked his daughter tersely.

'I didn't think you'd be doing *this,* she spat. 'How can you, Nick? How can you?' A savage scowl contorted her face and she looked at Briony with malevolent fury. 'And you had no right encouraging him.'

Briony stiffened and would have given the girl her answer if Nicholas hadn't got in first. 'That's enough, Jojo. This has nothing to do with you; please go back to your room.'

'I'm not a child,' she snapped. 'You can't order me around. I want to know what's going on. Do you intend having an affair with this woman?'

'Jojo, I want no more of this,' he warned tersely, finally letting Briony go.

She left the room quickly. Jo's interruption had brought her to her senses, made her see that it had been a grave mistake in the first place to let him anywhere near. His daughter was probably right—he was after an affair, amusing himself at her expense until he had completed his search for the will.

Angry with both herself and Nicholas, she ran up to her room and locked the door. Never would she let herself be led into such a compromising situation again. It had been totally embarrassing, made worse by Jo's obvious revulsion.

Did she always throw such tantrums if her father entertained another woman? Did she want no one to take the place of the mother she had never known? The fact that Nicholas had shown her photographs of Leonora and talked about her at length probably did not help. It might have been better had he not mentioned Jo's mother at all. The girl had grown up with a fixed idea in her mind of what her mother was like and wanted no one to replace her.

What were they talking about now? Was Nicholas explaining his feelings, whatever they might be, or was he telling his daughter to mind her own business? She really was a difficult girl and it possibly all boiled down to the fact that he had brought her up alone. No doubt she had frequently been left to her own devices, got her own way a lot of the time, and when she didn't it was a battle royal!

Briony stayed in her room for the rest of the day. She knew it was stupid being a prisoner in her own home, but she did not want to see Nicholas again. The next morning, after an almost sleepless night, she was down making herself a cup of tea at six o'clock. She was not altogether surprised when Nicholas joined her. He had this unnerving habit of creeping up on her, finding her wherever she was, upsetting her equilibrium.

'Good morning, good morning,' he greeted her cheerfully. 'I'm sorry about yesterday. I've told Jojo she must apologise to you.' He was wearing a black tracksuit with a silver trim, the open zip on the top revealing an almost hairless chest, which surprised her. His hair grew so thickly on his head that she had thought his body would be similarly covered. Nevertheless his skin was deeply tanned and she had the insane urge to run her fingertips over it.

'I don't want her apologies.' She deliberately made her tone hard. 'It's yours I need. I'm not surprised she was disgusted. I must have been out of my mind to let you anywhere near, let alone go as far as you did.'

His head jerked and he looked at her sharply. 'I gained the impression that you were enjoying it.'

'I foolishly got carried away,' she admitted, 'but it was a heat-of-the-moment thing. It was utter madness and I have no intention of letting it happen again.'

'You were missing Paul and felt frustrated, perhaps?' he jeered. 'Did you imagine I was your boyfriend? Was it his image in your mind when you whimpered your pleasure?'

Briony curled up inside with humiliation. 'As a matter of fact, yes, it was,' she lied, thankful of the excuse. 'I cannot wait for him to come home.'

Nicholas's jaw tightened and there was a fierce light in his eyes as he made himself a mug of coffee with the water left in the kettle. 'I refuse to be made a fool of, Briony,' he grated.

'Is your daughter starting college today?' she asked, anxious to change the subject.

He inclined his head. 'Much against her will. She wanted another week to settle in, but I didn't think it was good for her having nothing to do. Would you like to come jogging with me?'

Briony shook her head.

'Don't you exercise at all?'

'Of course I do. I swim, I go to aerobics once a week; I think that's enough.'

He nodded. 'Perhaps you could take Jojo with you?'

'I don't think she'd like that,' said Briony at once. 'She's resented me right from the beginning, probably even more so after last night.'

'It was a pity,' he agreed, his mouth twisting ruefully. 'I was beginning to enjoy it. We'll have to be more careful next time.'

'Next time?' Briony's eyes widened angrily. 'Let me tell you here and now—there won't be a next time. I'll never make such a foolish mistake again.'

CHAPTER SEVEN

IN THE days that followed Briony tried her hardest to ignore Nicholas and his daughter. Sometimes she succeeded, though more often than not he insisted on spending his evenings with her. He seemed to be doing his best to be friendly, even though she made it very clear that she did not want his company.

One day she came home from the office to discover that he had prepared a meal for them all. Up until now he had been very good, obeying her wishes and eating separately. She could not think why he had chosen to cook a communal meal on this occasion.

Nevertheless it was delicious: spare ribs of pork cooked in a sherry and pineapple sauce, served with egg fried rice and an assortment of dishes containing coconut, sultanas, et cetera. Briony had always been a fan of Chinese food, but he wasn't to know that and she thought he had taken quite a risk.

Once the meal was over Josephine departed to watch television and Briony helped Nicholas clear the table. 'That was a most enjoyable meal, thank you. I had no idea you were such a good cook.'

He shrugged. 'I can turn my hand to most things, and you don't have to do this, you know. This evening is my treat.'

A rare treat indeed. No one ever cooked for her. Paul still lived at home with his mother, his father having died many years earlier, and the older woman did everything for him. In fact Briony sometimes wondered whether she was the reason he had never got round to seriously discussing marriage. He was always saying that his mother couldn't cope on her own, but Briony saw her as a very possessive woman who treated Paul as though he were still a schoolboy. Goodness knew how she felt when he was away on one of his courses.

After she had loaded the dishes into the dishwasher and the kitchen was neat and tidy, Nicholas suggested they sit for a while in the conservatory. 'There's a full moon tonight; if we're lucky we might see some wildlife,' he told her. 'I can remember as a child seeing my first fox. I was terribly excited, and after that I saw him often, and hedgehogs and shrews and mice. My father used to sit with me and point them out. He was an incredibly patient man.'

'And were you patient?' she asked as they sat down.

'Not so much then as I am now.' Although she could not see the expression in his eyes there was something in his tone which suggested that he was no longer talking about animals.

Briony had the feeling that it was going to be an uncomfortable evening, that the camaraderie she had felt during dinner was already a thing of the past. He had one thing firmly fixed in his mind, and that was to develop some sort of relationship with her, something to while away the time until he had sorted things out to his own satisfaction as far as Thornton Hall was concerned.

'Have you found out what went wrong with your father's business?' she asked, anxious to keep the conversation on an impersonal level.

He inclined his head. 'I've had some luck. A guy at one of the companies who used to be a customer of my father remembers him very well and said he could never understand why they suddenly stopped placing orders with him. He's promised to look into things, find out what happened.'

'I hate to think that your father's downfall was a deliberate plot,' said Briony.

'And caused by my own stupidity,' he hissed. 'If I hadn't phoned Cameron it wouldn't have happened. I hold myself entirely to blame, and I'll never rest until I've got to the bottom of it and seen justice done.'

'The feud will never die if you do that.'

'As if I care,' he tossed savagely. 'I shall avenge my father's destruction if it's the last thing I do. But let's not spoil tonight with such thoughts; let's enjoy our time together.'

'How can I enjoy myself with the enemy?' she spat, putting far more vengeance into her tone than she felt. 'You and I will never become friends.' Briony's eyes had grown accustomed to the darkness and in the light from the moon she could see Nicholas's face clearly. It was becoming increasingly familiar and although she always felt nervous when they spent time together she felt an incredible awareness too. No matter how much she told herself she hated him, the feelings were always there. She was actually beginning to crave some sort of fulfillment. It was madness, and if he touched her she knew she would fight him off, and yet...

'I was thinking of something rather more than friends,' he said with a slow smile.

She looked at him sharply. 'I think you're forgetting Paul.' And so was she, if the truth were known. Nicholas filled her thoughts almost to the exclusion of all else. It was wrong, and she must put a stop to it.

'How could I forget the man who means more to you than anyone else in the world?' he asked drily. 'But as he's not here, as he seems to think nothing of deserting you for days—or is it weeks?—at a time, he can't think very much of you. If the guy loved you he'd be on the phone every spare moment he had. You can't be serious about him?'

'Of course I'm serious.' But she did not look at him as she answered.

'Then I shall look forward to meeting this guy whom you hold in such high esteem. He must be someone very special for you to have waited patiently for six whole years for a marriage proposal. How much longer do you think he'll keep you waiting?'

Briony shot him an angry glance. 'It's no business of yours.'

'But I'd like it to be. At the risk of becoming a bore, I'll repeat that I'm very attracted to you, and I promise I could offer you far more than your extremely dull insurance friend.'

'In what way?' she snapped. 'And please don't talk like that about someone you don't know.'

'For instance you wouldn't have to lose this house; there's room for all of us.'

Briony glared, hating the thought of sharing with him on a permanent basis. 'I have no intention of losing the house anyway,' she spat.

'You were going to sell it,' he pointed out.

'Only because circumstances were forcing me to.'

'And your circumstances have changed. Is that what you're trying to tell me?' His eyes were narrowed and watchful on hers, seeming to see right into her mind, knowing that everything was exactly the same as it had been before he erupted into her life.

'I'll find a way to keep it,' she muttered fiercely.

'Anything to stop me from moving in?' There was a sudden savage edge to his tone, his jaw rigid. 'Do you really hate me so much that you'd cause yourself suffering to stop me from taking over?'

'Yes.' Maybe she didn't exactly hate him, but it was his attitude that got her back up. Why should she give in to him? Why let him get the house?

Her single quiet word of admission made him bellow with anger. 'I can see why my father changed his will—you're not worthy of his generosity. You're nothing but a selfish little bitch.'

Briony gasped and reeled back in her seat as though he had struck her. 'How dare you speak to me like that? James and I got on extremely well. He said more than once that I was like a real daughter to him. It's quite obvious, by the fact that he said he had no children, that he had washed his hands of you completely. He must have had a mental aberration when he sent that letter, changing his mind immediately afterwards.' She was breathing heavily now, completely incensed by his attitude.

'And you feel that you are doing the right thing by stopping me getting it?' The skin was drawn tightly across his face, the pale light of the moon accentuating even more dramatically its harsh angles.

'I'm sure your father didn't have it in mind for you to turn up and throw me out.'

His eyes narrowed. 'I have never said that. In fact I think I'm being more than generous by saying that you can share the house with Jojo and me.'

'Really generous,' she scorned. 'And you'd make my life such hell that I'd be glad to get out. Don't think I can't see through you. The only interests you've got at heart are your own.'

'So it's me who's the selfish bastard, is it?' He sprang to his feet and stood looking menacingly down at her.

'I've had enough of this.' Briony bounced up too. 'I'm going up to my room.'

'I think we should go for a walk.'

Briony looked at him sharply, warily. There was already a different inflexion in his voice. Gone was the anger, or at least on the surface; he sounded almost friendly again.

'It's a perfect night,' he added persuasively. 'Why don't you fetch your coat?'

A perfect night for what?' thought Briony. For lovers? What could be more romantic than walking beneath a star-spangled sky and a moon so luminous that it touched everything with silver? But it was not for her, not with Nicholas. It was a recipe for disaster.

He growled impatiently as she dithered. 'What the hell is wrong now?'

'I was thinking that I can't see any point in it,' she said with some exasperation. 'All we'll do is carry on arguing.'

'Not necessarily. I've had my say; I'm not one to drag out arguments.' And to her amazement he suddenly smiled.

Reluctantly Briony found herself agreeing, even though she knew she was mad for doing so.

They walked side by side, pausing when they heard the hoot of an owl somewhere in the garden. There was a chill in the air and she pushed her hands deep into the pockets of her anorak and tried to concentrate on her surroundings rather than the man at her side.

It was difficult, especially when he walked so close that they were almost touching. They were not walking fast and yet she felt breathless, her whole body alive and aware and totally responsive. In fact the moonlight added an extra dimension to her feelings. It was not something she could actually describe, but it was there and she knew that if he touched her now all would be lost.

But surprisingly he didn't. He looked at her often, and he smiled, and the anger seemed to have gone out of him, but he left her strictly alone. Contrarily Briony felt disappointed. 'I imagine you find it very cold here compared to Houston?' she asked, determined to find some sort of neutral conversation.

'Indeed I do, but I nevertheless love it here. If I hadn't been so tied up in my job, if it hadn't meant so much to me, I'd have probably come home before now. I wish I had,' he added quietly, and Briony knew he was thinking about his father.

'I know nothing at all about oil,' she said, 'only what I've seen on television. Did you ever have a blow-out?'

Once Nicholas started talking there was no stopping him. He made everything sound fascinating and time went so quickly that when they reached the outskirts of the village Briony was surprised how far they had walked. 'I think we should go back now,' she said, slowing her steps.

'I thought we might have a drink somewhere?'

'No, thank you,' she replied, shaking her head emphatically.

'You've had enough of my company, is that what you're saying?' he asked, his tone sharp again.

'That's one of the reasons, yes, but I'm tired now; I want to get home and go to bed.' His moods swung like a pendulum from one extreme to the other, with scarcely any provocation.

He shot a glance at his watch. 'It's only ten o'clock, and I certainly haven't had enough of *your* company.' He halted outside the Red Lion, Tissingdale's only pub. 'We'll have one and then I promise we'll go back.' When he caught her elbow in a grip that threatened to paralyse, Briony had no choice.

The warm, cheerful atmosphere of the pub greeted them and the first person she saw was a fellow insurance salesman of Paul's. She wondered why he wasn't at the seminar too and groaned inwardly, mentally crossing her fingers that the news that she was out with another man would not reach Paul before she could explain herself.

The man acknowledged her but went on drinking with his companions and she and Nicholas moved on. It was busy and there were no seats and Briony found herself being constantly pushed up against Nicholas. She drank her vodka and blackcurrant quickly in the hope that they would leave.

'There's a certain atmosphere in an English country pub that you don't get anywhere else in the world,' he said, and he looked as though he was prepared to stay until closing time. 'Another drink?'

Briony shook her head.

'Now that's a pity, because I fancy one myself.'

'I think you drink too much,' she snapped.

Nicholas frowned. 'I've had one drink and we had nothing with our meal; what are you talking about?'

'You finished your father's whisky very quickly.'

His head jerked. 'That was because I needed it when I realised what Cameron had been up to. Dammit, Briony, I'm no more a drinking man than my father was—unless he changed over the years?'

She shook her head. 'He never drank much, not even when the going got hard. He had one small whisky each night, that was all.'

Nicholas nodded. 'He used to say to me, "Moderation in all things", and it's something I've lived by. But another drink won't hurt either of us. What's the rush?'

In the end they were in the pub until closing time and when they got outside it was to find that the weather had changed; the moon had disappeared, and it had begun to drizzle. 'I think maybe we should get a taxi,' said Nicholas, pulling up the collar of his jacket.

At that moment a minicab came cruising past and Nicholas put two fingers in his mouth and let out a piercing whistle. To Briony's amazement it stopped. Usually you had to phone for a cab in Tissingdale; it wasn't like London or any other big town or city. Briony was not even sure that they were supposed to stop, though it did not surprise her. Nicholas had that indefinable charismatic something that made people think, even at a glance, he was someone of power and importance.

He touched her elbow as he ushered her inside and an immediate jolt of electricity ran through her. They had spent so many hours together that it was inevitable her awareness of him had developed into an almost feverish intensity. Even so, she moved to the far side of the car.

Nicholas sat with a faint smile on his lips, as though he knew what she was thinking and feeling, knew that her body ached for his touch, and he was taking some sort of perverse delight in leaving her alone.

Until they got indoors! Once the front door closed behind them Briony headed straight for the stairs. 'Thank you for the meal and the drinks,' she called over her shoulder.

'Is that all I'm going to get? No goodnight kiss?' Nicholas's gruff voice halted her. 'That's hardly playing the game fair, is it?'

'It's not a game to me,' she snapped, turning briefly to look at him. 'It's an ordeal, as well you know.'

In an instant Nicholas was at her side, their eyes on a level now, and she could see very clearly his thick lashes, which were enviably long, and the pure whites, and the dark brown which always looked black from a distance.

'An ordeal?' he barked, nostrils dilated as he controlled his anger. 'I don't agree and I think it definitely must be proved once and for all. I think, honey, that you're fighting the inevitable.'

When his arms came about her, when their two mouths met, Briony was instantly lost. When their bodies came together every good intention failed, Nicholas's hard and strong and more masculine than any man she had ever met, her own soft and yielding and delicately perfumed, and definitely in danger of giving away the feverish, aching need that burnt inside her.

Although the hands that held her were iron-clad, his lips grazed hers so softly that the kiss was all the more erotic because of it. Gently, oh, so gently, tiny butterfly kisses on the corners of her mouth, on her cheeks, the tip of her nose, her eyelids, moving with painful slowness to the lobes of her ears and the soft, incredibly sensitive skin behind.

Without being conscious of it Briony gyrated her hips against him and with a faint groan his mouth claimed hers again, moving more urgently this time, his tongue tasting and feeling the contours of her lips, probing and parting. Her unsteady heartbeats echoed inside her head, pulses quickened, and she gave her mouth up to his in complete surrender. Her traitorous body had been waiting and wanting and actually needing this moment all evening.

'What the hell is going on?'

The male voice was instantly recognisable and Briony jerked herself guiltily free. 'Paul! I didn't know you were back!' By his side stood a smiling Josephine, and it was obvious by her triumphant expression that she had planned this moment deliberately.

'Obviously,' he grated. Not so tall as Nicholas, tow-headed, blue-eyed, usually mildly mannered, but at this moment his face red with anger, his blue eyes blazing. 'I think I deserve an explanation.'

'Paul.' Briony took a step towards him then stopped. 'I—er—this is Nicholas Grant. We——'

'I know who he is,' growled Paul. 'What I want to know is what's going on between you two?'

'Nothing's going on,' she protested at once.

Paul snorted derisively. 'How can you say that after what I've just observed.'

'Briony wasn't the instigator of that little scene; she was a very reluctant participant.' Nicholas strode towards the smaller man and held out his hand. 'You must be Paul Holman; Briony's told me about you.'

Paul ignored the outstretched hand. 'Briony did not look as though she was being forced into anything. In fact she——'

'Paul!' Briony looked at him pleadingly. 'Can't we discuss this in private?'

'I don't think there's anything to discuss,' he answered coldly. 'From what I've seen you've made it very clear that you prefer this man to me. I'm disappointed in you, Briony, I really am. I thought we had something good going for us; I thought I could trust you. I never expected to return and find you two-timing me.'

'I'm not.' She moved to him and touched her hand to his arm. 'It was nothing, I assure you, a thank you for an evening out, that's all.'

'It looked like a mighty big thank you to me. What were you doing going out with him in the first place?'

'Instead of condemning Briony you should be thanking me for looking after her.' Nicholas looked at the other man condescendingly. 'No man in his right mind would leave such an attractive girl for such a length of time without so much as a phone call. My God, man, you deserve to lose her.'

Briony groaned silently and closed her eyes for a fleeting moment. Trust Nicholas to make things worse.

'Briony and I have an understanding,' Paul told him pompously.

'Yes, I know, a six-year one.' Nicholas's voice was filled with scorn. 'What sort of man are you to keep a girl dangling for all that time?'

'*Nicholas*!' protested Briony furiously. 'You have no right saying things like that.' Even though her feelings for Paul had waned considerably she still would not hear him spoken to like this.

'It's the truth, isn't it?' the dark-haired man asked unrepentantly. 'The way I see things, Paul doesn't care enough about you to warrant any loyalty at all.'

Briony was incensed. 'Whatever you think it doesn't give you any right to criticise my friend. Kindly leave us; I'd like to speak to Paul alone.'

'Very well.'

She was surprised when Nicholas agreed so readily, but shocked beyond measure when he muttered gruffly in her ear, 'I haven't forgotten where we got to; we'll carry on afterwards.'

She wanted to come back with a sharp retort, but as it appeared that Paul, fortunately, hadn't heard Nicholas's low words she had to be satisfied with a glowering glance and a grim tightening of her lips.

Nicholas took his daughter's arm and they both disappeared, though Briony guessed they wouldn't be far away. Josephine was enjoying the situation she had created and Nicholas was quite ready to do battle with Paul.

She turned to Paul, who was watching her stonily. 'I'm sorry about this; it's not how it looked. Nicholas Grant is a hateful person, I——'

'How can it not be how it looked?' he asked bitterly. 'I stood watching you kissing him and you certainly did not act like a girl being forced into something against her will.'

'You don't know what he's like,' she said. 'He can be very persuasive.'

'I bet he can. He's a much better catch than I am, isn't he? Wealthy for a start, and if he really is the rightful owner of this place then you're made for life, aren't you?'

She was astonished that Paul had summed up the situation so quickly and so accurately. 'I could be, but I don't plan to be,' she answered sharply. 'Nicholas Grant is not my type; I hate him, and I did everything in my power to stop him moving in.'

'And yet you still went out with him tonight?'

'As far as I was concerned we were only going for a walk after our meal, but then he insisted on dropping in at the Red Lion for a drink. I didn't want to, I assure you.'

Paul looked at her doubtfully. 'He's a handsome guy.'

'I've told you, he's not my type.'

'Are you sure about that, Briony?' His blue eyes were disturbed as he looked at her contemplatively. 'His daughter told me that you two have got pretty friendly.'

'Josephine would say anything,' she retorted. 'The girl resents me; she thinks I shouldn't be in this house, that it should rightfully belong to them.'

'I must confess I was surprised when she told me the situation.'

'No more than I was,' returned Briony. 'I could not believe it—I still don't, as a matter of fact. There's no trace of a second will; I think Nicholas is making it up.'

'So what's the position? How long is he likely to remain here?' Paul looked slightly more relaxed, but not very much, and he made no attempt to touch her.

'Forever if he has his way,' she told him tightly. 'We're waiting for James's solicitor to come back from holiday and sort things out. He's the only one who'll be able to confirm that Nicholas Grant is who he says he is, but, as for another will, I'm sure he doesn't know about that—and after all this time I don't see why Nicholas should have any claim on this place.'

'But you were going to sell,' he reminded her.

Briony nodded. 'I still will; the trouble is prospective purchasers aren't actually queueing up at the door. The last person who came Nicholas saw off pretty sharply.'

'And you let him?'

'Not willingly,' she replied, 'but he seems to have a knack of always getting his own way.'

'Like stealing my girlfriend off me?'

Briony shook her head. 'He hasn't done that.'

'But he's close to it? It appears I came back just in time.'

'Why didn't you phone me?'

'Because it was hectic. We didn't have a second to ourselves, except to sleep, and you know I'd never ring you late at night. I thought you'd understand.'

'I bet you phoned your mother?'

He looked slightly taken aback. 'Well, of course, but that's different, she worries so.'

Didn't he think she worried? It was evident that their relationship had gone stale, that he took her very much for granted, and she ought to put an end to it right now, but instead she said nothing, and an awkward little silence developed between them.

'What are you doing tomorrow night?' he asked. 'We could go out for a quiet meal somewhere; we have a lot to talk about.'

Briony did not see how it would solve anything, but she inclined her head nevertheless. 'I'd like that, but don't you usually work on weekday evenings?'

'I think I deserve some time off after all the hours I've put in lately. I'll phone in sick; you're more important to me than my job. I'll pick you up at seven-thirty.'

It was the first time he had ever put her before work. The shock of seeing her with Nicholas had obviously done some good. She followed him to the door and didn't know whether she was disappointed or relieved when all he did was peck her cheek before stepping outside. She watched until he had gone and then locked and bolted the door. To her annoyance, when she turned, Nicholas

Grant was standing watching her, a cynical smile of pleasure on his face.

'I was right, he is a wimp.'

'How dare you?' Briony was up in arms immediately.

'The least he could have done was punch my jaw. I know that's what I'd have done if someone stole my girl.'

'You haven't stolen me,' she reminded him.

'But I was on the verge of it. Your boyfriend has terrible timing. He interrupted what set out to be a very promising evening.'

'And I'm glad that he did,' she spat savagely. 'I must have been out of my mind to let you anywhere near me.'

'Briony.' He wagged a finger at her. 'You know that isn't true. You were enjoying it just as much as I was. For the first time you were letting yourself go, forgetting that I was the enemy and accepting me for what I really am.'

'Rubbish!' cried Briony furiously, her grey eyes flashing sparks of fire.

'So what was the reason for the sudden capitulation?'

His knowing smile irritated her even further and she shook her head savagely. 'I don't have to answer these questions; I'm going to bed. Goodnight.'

But it was not so easy. With one sideways step he barred her path. 'You've been struck with an attack of guilt, is that it? Dear Paul has returned and you've realised where your loyalties lie?'

'Yes, as a matter of fact,' she told him tightly, standing tall, her chin jutting, yet even at the same time feeling the full impact of him. Loyalties faded into nothingness where this man was concerned. He triggered every one of her senses into exciting, vibrant life and she wanted him with a desperation that appalled her. Paul had been gone a matter of minutes and here she was hungering after another man. It was madness, insanity; she was out of her mind.

There was no way she could step round him to go up-stairs and she knew without a shadow of doubt that if she attempted to push past he would pull her into his arms and all would be lost. So she turned instead and headed for the kitchen.

His strong, deep voice reached out to her. 'Where are you going?'

'To make myself a hot drink,' she flung over her shoulder.

'A good idea, I think I'll join you.'

Briony tensed and halted and swung round to face him. 'Are you so insensitive that you can't see I'm trying to get away from you?'

His smile was slow and merciless. 'I know exactly what you're doing.'

'Then why can't you leave me alone?'

'For the simple reason I don't want to. I meant what I said, Briony, about carrying on where we left off. Whether it's sooner or later is up to you.'

Her eyes blazed, even at the same time as nerve-endings tingled and pulses ran amok. 'I shan't make that mistake again,' she told him, shaking her head slowly and deliberately.

'It wasn't a mistake, Briony. You were following your natural instincts, and surely that's what it's all about?'

'I love Paul,' she defended herself.

Thick black brows shot up. 'I didn't notice you run into his arms, and his goodnight kiss was purely perfunctory.'

'You were watching!' she accused.

'A very interested bystander, and my deductions are that whatever you once had going between you is long since dead. Life needs a little excitement, something to get the blood tingling through your veins. There'd be none of that with Holman.'

The fact that he was right inflamed Briony even further. 'How can you make such sweeping statements when you don't even know Paul?'

'What little I saw was enough to convince that he's not the man for you.'

'And you are, I suppose; is that what you're saying?'

'I'm saying that life with me would never be dull.'

'No, because we'd be arguing all the time,' she returned sharply. 'Don't think I don't know that you're hedging your bets in case the will isn't found, but it won't work.'

'You think that I . . .' He paused and gave a bark of laughter.

'You can mock,' she spat. 'You can deny it all you like, but I won't believe you. You want Thornton Hall and you're determined to get it by fair means or foul.'

His lips twisted wryly. 'You're so beautiful.'

'And you're a monster and I hate you.'

'Really?' He moved closer to her. 'I'm not used to girls saying they hate me. Perhaps you're confused? Perhaps what you really feel is——?'

'No!' cut in Briony savagely.

'I think you should let me be the best judge of that.'

Briony knew she ought to turn and run, but his black eyes were on hers, mesmerising, drawing her to him against her will, rekindling the feelings of a few minutes earlier. When his hands touched her arms she knew it was too late, and her cries of protest were faint as his mouth swooped down on hers.

CHAPTER EIGHT

BRIONY astonished herself by making no demur when Nicholas swung her up into his arms and, with lips still clinging, carried her upstairs and along the corridor to her room. The door was kicked open and closed behind them, she was put back on her feet, and still their mouths clung.

It was one of the headiest sensations of Briony's life. She felt as though she were drinking the sweet nectar of life from his mouth; it was running like fire through her veins, affecting her like ten-year-old brandy, intoxicating, exhilarating—debilitating! Almost knocking her off her feet. Paul was forgotten, completely.

It was a kiss to surpass all kisses and went on so long that time lost all meaning. It was as if they had waited so long for this moment that neither was prepared to let the other go.

Finally, reluctantly, Nicholas lifted his head from hers, cupping her face between his hard-boned hands and looking deeply into the luminous, turbulent depths of her smoky grey eyes. She was unaware how soft they had gone, how much they told him; she knew only that her own desire was mirrored in his.

'Briony.' His tone was harsh and low. 'Oh, Briony, what you do to me.' A gentle fingertip traced the bow of her lips. 'I did not want to stop.'

'So why did you?' she asked huskily. Her throat was so dry she could hardly talk—even swallowing was difficult—and she failed to understand how one single, though admittedly long kiss could do this to her. There was no rhyme nor reason behind it. And it was only the tip of the iceberg! If Nicholas chose to prolong their lovemaking, to take things further, to touch her breasts, to kiss them, to suck her nipples into his mouth, to... She dared not think any further. The excitement caused her adrenalin to run high and she did not realise that all this time she had been sinking and drowning in Nicholas's rich black eyes.

'It doesn't pay to hurry,' he murmured thickly. 'Love-making needs to be savoured, every moment tasted and enjoyed.'

Briony agreed with him. It was a point of view she had never considered before, but there was absolutely no doubt that she had enjoyed his kiss, was still enjoying it! She could still feel his mouth on hers, could still taste his essential maleness, still felt buoyed up.

This wasn't what it was all supposed to be about. She ought to be fending him off instead of revelling in his kisses, her body should be rejecting instead of wel-coming—there was Paul to think of; and yet even though they were no longer kissing she still felt aroused, still wanted him, wanted more.

In one respect she felt ashamed of these wanton feelings surging and spiralling inside her, and in another she decided that if it felt this good then it couldn't be wrong. And so long as she didn't lose her head, didn't let things get out of hand, what did a few minutes' pleasure matter? All she needed to do was make sure that she did not compromise herself to the extent that Nicholas got the upper hand.

Paul had never, in the whole of the time she had been going out with him, given her such pleasure, and she knew it was time to bring their relationship to a close. If excitement like this could be combined with real love, then that would be something worth having. Not that she was ever likely to fall in love with Nicholas, but with someone else who had the power to arouse her to these same ecstatic heights—after just a kiss!

His hands moved from her face to trail slowly down her throat, pausing momentarily to touch the throbbing, tell-tale pulse at its base, then over the aching curves of her breasts—all the time their eyes locked together. She expected and wanted more, wanted him to hold her breasts, but he continued his descent, moulding her waist and hips, feeling the soft feminine shape of her, and then—and only then—did he work his hands up beneath her fine wool sweater.

At his touch on her bare skin she drew in a rasping breath of pleasure, and he saw and heard and his eyes shadowed a similar response. Sheer, sweet ecstasy, too much to bear. She closed her eyes and her head fell back on her shoulders and when he lifted her sweater she willingly let him pull it off altogether. Her white lace bra was dispensed with equally swiftly and he stood a moment just looking at her, his fingertips tracing her outline with a sort of reverence that she found amazing.

Everything about this man surprised her. He was tough and arrogant and utterly ruthless at times, and yet he could be so gentle, so—so—she could not find the word, but, whatever, it was this side of him that aroused her deepest emotions.

She stood while he reverently touched and moulded and looked at her breasts. 'You're so lovely, Briony,' he muttered, 'so perfect.' He took the full weight of each breast into his palms and rubbed his thumbs over her nipples, inducing incredible sensations not only in her breasts but through the whole of her body. Dear heaven, what sweet pleasure.

He sat her on the edge of the bed and knelt before her so that he could take each nipple in turn into his mouth. There was no haste in his movements; he was savouring each second, as she was herself, and each action was deliberate—he knew exactly what he was doing to her, knew the tremendous excitement that was careering wildly through her veins. It was a long, slow torture, inducing her into a state of frenzy that she found difficult to curb.

Be careful, she warned herself; don't let things get out of hand, don't forget that all you're after is a few minutes' pleasure. Pleasure of the sort no other man had ever given her!

It made her realise what a waste all the years she had spent with Paul were. Many of her friends had told her that he wasn't right for her, but she had always said that they didn't know what they were talking about, that she loved Paul and always would.

No longer did she think this way. A few hours of this man's company had changed all that—not that she would ever let Nicholas know this. Paul was her defence—or had been until this moment. She wondered what Nicholas was thinking, whether he wondered whether she did this sort of thing with Paul?

As if reading her thoughts, he lifted his head. 'I guess Paul's a lucky guy. How he could go away and leave you I have no idea. I would never do that if you were mine.'

'Didn't Leonora leave you because you spent more time at work than you did with her? Wasn't that the cause of your problems?' she asked, glad of these few moments' respite.

'I was young and inexperienced then,' he answered gruffly, sitting back on his heels and looking up at her. 'I did a lot of things I wouldn't do now.'

'Have you ever thought of trying to find her? Apart from that time you rang Charles Cameron?'

He shook his head. 'Whatever feelings I had for her are dead; perhaps I never truly loved her. The opposition from our parents pushed us together. We were young and foolish and thought we knew best. And what are we doing talking about Leonora when it's you I'm with? You really are incredible, Briony. Is it any wonder I'm bowled over by you?'

Before she could toss scorn on to his statement he was on his feet and with the gentlest of touches on her shoulders had laid her down on the bed. What was more amazing, she let him. She really ought to be struggling now, but somehow every ounce of resistance had fled; she actually wanted this intimacy, needed it, even.

She closed her eyes and felt his mouth on her breasts and again time lost all meaning—until his hand slid beneath her skirt. 'No!' Her hand came on top of his and stopped him. 'No, Nicholas, not that.'

His eyes, his beautifully long-lashed eyes, narrowed fractionally. 'You can't stop me now.'

'I can and I will,' she told him firmly.

'But you want this as much as me, you've proved it.'

'No, I don't,' she denied, her mouth set mutinously. 'I've enjoyed being kissed by you, but I refuse to let it go any further.'

His eyes narrowed dangerously. 'I could take you if I wanted to.'

'If you want to be accused of rape, yes.'

'It wouldn't be rape, and you know it,' he told her harshly.

Briony realised that it had been a grave mistake letting him into her room. She had given him the wrong idea, and now, if she was not careful, she would pay for it. She sat up and pulled the sheet quickly over her. 'I'd like you to go.' She had hoped to inject a note of authority into her voice; instead it came out wavery and troubled.

'You mean you think it would be the right and proper thing to do?' He stood up, but he did not move away from the bed, and his powerful presence still blazed down over her.

Briony inclined her head, not trusting herself to speak again. This was agony of the worst kind. She had denied her own basic needs by rejecting him; they still raged inside her, yet she knew that she had done the right thing. Letting him make love would give him the hold over her that he wanted. She knew exactly what he was up to; his actions were purely selfish, his feelings lacking emotion of any kind.

'You disappoint me, Briony.'

'Maybe,' she shrugged, 'but that's the way it's going to be.'

'We'll see. Maybe I rushed you, maybe I should have waited until you gave Paul his marching orders.'

'What do you mean?' asked Briony sharply.

'Surely that is what you're going to do? I don't care what you say—you don't love the guy, and he sure as hell doesn't love you. You've just settled into this relationship and the sooner you get out of it the better.'

Briony glared. 'You know nothing.'

'I know more than you think. I'm not blind, honey. I saw for myself the way you two reacted to each other— and it certainly wasn't with love.'

'That's because Paul saw me with you. How did you expect him to behave?'

'As I said before, he should have laid into me. He's too weak for you, Briony. You're a strong, independent woman; you'd be bored out of your pretty mind within weeks if you married him. You need someone like me who draws the best out in you.'

'Or the worst,' she riposted.

'Even the worst is better than indifference—and that's what he feels. Give him up, Briony. Tell him tomorrow night that it's all over.'

'You were listening!' she accused.

'Indeed, and I have no intention of apologising for doing so.'

'You bastard! Get out!' Briony sprang from the bed and marched across the room, yanking open the door and holding it open for him to leave.

He strolled slowly towards her, smiling maddeningly. 'You're so beautiful; is it any wonder I'm half in love with you?'

Briony closed her eyes so that she would not see him, but knew it was a mistake when she felt his lips brush over hers. She flicked her lids open and found herself looking into the black velvet depths of his eyes, and the whole world began to spin. She held on to the door and made herself say harshly, 'You're insane. The only person you're in love with is yourself. Everything you're doing is for yourself. You're the most selfish person I've ever met.'

Muscles jerked in his jaw and his eyes lost their softness, grew hard and dangerous. 'I don't care for accusations of that kind, Briony.'

'Not even when they're the truth?' she retorted.

'It would appear that you haven't learned anything about me yet.'

'Only that you're despicable. Now get out.'

Their eyes locked and warred and Briony knew that all would be lost if he did not go quickly. She had no doubt that he was well aware of her real emotions and were he to ignore her objections, wrap her once again into his arms, all the fight would go out of her.

'I'll go,' he said softly, 'but I can't promise this won't happen again. Indeed, I know it will. You're irresistible, Briony, and I'm quite sure that if Paul hadn't turned up tonight you wouldn't have stopped me. My advice is to sort yourself out with him quickly.'

'If you think that you'll benefit from it, then you're wrong,' she snapped. 'Even if I did finish with Paul—

which I don't intend to—then I still wouldn't enter into an affair with you. That's the last thing I want.'

His lips quirked. 'We'll see. Goodnight, Briony, sleep well.'

How would she ever do that? she thought as he closed the door silently behind him. He had come so close to winning tonight; she hated herself for being so weak. Yet even so she still felt a warm glow inside her. None of that had gone away. Her body still craved fulfilment, still crazily needed him. She had never known that physical desire could cause such pain.

Angrily she jumped to her feet and stripped off the rest of her clothes. In the bathroom she stood beneath the powerful jets of the shower, desperately needing to wash the feel of him off her, and yet, conversely, as she soaped her skin it was as though it were his hands touching her, his hands stroking and inducing mindless sensations. She had never felt such an awareness of her own body before and she felt deeply troubled.

The feelings continued throughout the rest of the night, keeping her restless and awake, and the times her hands roved to touch her breasts, to experience again those selfsame feelings, were innumerable. She began to wonder what was the matter with her, why she couldn't forget the whole episode and push it right out of her mind.

She felt dreadful, as though she was betraying Paul, and yet Nicholas was right: she did not love him any more and it was doubtful that whatever Paul felt for her was as strong as it should be for a happy marriage.

When morning dawned she determinedly did not go downstairs until it was time to leave for the office, not feeling up to facing Nicholas again so soon. She ought to have known, however, that she would not get away with it. He was waiting for her in the tiled hallway.

When he saw her with her coat on and her bag in her hand he frowned. 'What's this, no breakfast this morning?'

'I overslept,' she lied. 'I haven't time.'

'It's not good for you,' he warned. '*I* wouldn't have anything to do with your decision to forgo breakfast, by any chance?' There was a glimmer in his eyes that told her he knew the truth.

'Why should you?' she asked coolly, at the same time a torrent of hot emotions raging inside her. She would never be able to face him again without this surge of need. God, please let Richard Brent return quickly and get rid of this man, she prayed. I cannot go through this every day for the next week and a half. It will kill me.

'I was just wondering,' he answered with assumed innocence. 'After all, we did get rather intense last night—until you put a stop to it. I know I for one am still feeling the effects.'

His confession startled Briony and she felt a faint frown forming on her brow. This did not equate with her thoughts of him. Unless he was saying it to make her feel good, to pave the way for a repeat performance? This sounded a more likely explanation.

'Aren't you?' he asked, when she remained silent.

'Not at all,' she lied again.

'Are you feeling guilty because of Paul?'

She eyed him stonily. 'Naturally. I should never have let it happen.'

'But you did and you enjoyed it, probably more than you have ever enjoyed kissing Paul, so why the remorse? You know as well as I do that it's all over between you two.'

He looked and sounded so confident that Briony could have spat in his face. 'You know nothing of the sort; it's all what you'd like to think will happen, but it won't, and when I see Paul tonight I fully intend suggesting we make plans for our wedding.'

Now why had she said that? Briony was appalled to think that she had made such a rash statement. She must be careful that she did not let Nicholas bulldoze her into doing something she would later regret. The years she had spent loving Paul had been a complete waste of time; all she could be thankful for was that she had found out before it was too late. The irony was that it was this irritating stranger who had made her come to her senses. Nevertheless, it might be best if he thought she was serious; it might keep him off her back.

His face was forbidding, his eyes narrowed as he looked at her. 'I truly hope that you'll do nothing so foolish.'

'What I do is my own affair,' she tossed back. 'Now if you'll excuse me I should hate to be late for work.'

Briony found it incredibly difficult to concentrate, to the extent that her boss asked her if anything was wrong, and when she got home she could not believe her eyes when she found Nicholas hovering in the hall again.

He wore a black polo shirt and close-fitting black trousers—a lethal combination which set every one of her nerves tingling. Black suited him, made him mysterious and sexy, and very exciting. Nevertheless, she managed to inject a note of irritation into her voice. 'Can't you keep out of my way?'

'Now there's a greeting when I've been waiting for you for hours.'

Briony shook her head in exasperation. 'You're crazy, do you know that? When are you going to get it through your thick skull that I want nothing to do with you? That if I had my way you wouldn't be in this house at all?'

'The only thing I know is that you're irresistible.' His dark eyes held hers, sending urgent messages of desire, heightening the erotic sensations she was doing her very best to suppress.

It was so unfair, this hold he had over her. Having always prided herself on being in full control of her emotions, she found it disconcerting to be able to do nothing about them now. What was it about Nicholas that drew her to him like a moth to a flame, that made her find *him* irresistible?

'I think you're lying,' she snapped. 'We both know the reason you're chasing me and it has nothing to do with personalities.'

'You still think it's to make things easier for me to get my hands on Thornton Hall if the will should not turn up?'

'Isn't that true?' she snapped.

His mouth grew grim. 'It's a long way away from it. I never use people, Briony. Whatever gave you that idea?'

She lifted her shoulders in a defensive shrug. 'It's a logical conclusion. Why else would you claim to be attracted to me? Shouldn't I be your enemy?'

'How can such a beautiful lady be an enemy?' he countered. 'Admittedly I was stunned to find you in possession of my father's house, but admiration swiftly overcame prejudice.'

Briony did not believe him for one moment and she eyed him scornfully. 'I think this is enough of the Briony Weston Appreciation Society. I'm going up to take a shower and get changed before Paul gets here.'

'Wouldn't you rather be spending your evening with me?'

His insolence astonished her. 'No, indeed I would not,' she flashed.

'You cannot deny your very real response to me last night. Or was it simply a last fling before settling back into your boring routine with your equally boring lover?'

'God, I hate you,' cried Briony.

'The way I see it, there are three explanations for your behaviour. You're either a very sexy lady who cannot get enough of it——'

'*No*!' yelled Briony at once. Could he really think that of her?

'Or,' he went on, disregarding her outburst, 'it was frustration because Paul has been away for so long, and even when he turned up he did nothing about it. Or——' he gave a half smile as he looked at her '—and I think this is the most likely—your feelings for Paul are not what you think they are. In other words, you don't love him, no matter that you keep telling me to the contrary.'

'You don't know what you're talking about,' Briony spat, but there was not much conviction in her voice.

'Then you tell me why you responded so hungrily.' His dark eyes, as they so often were, were intent upon hers, stimulating and rousing and making it extremely difficult to give any coherent answer.

'I don't even know the answer myself,' she snapped. 'You're a very sexy man—I'll grant you that; you can make love to a woman without even touching her. No one could fail to respond when you set out to seduce.'

His lips quirked. 'So how come I didn't get very far?'

'Far enough, I would say. I do have some strength of character, though it would appear not enough.'

'What you're saying is that if I persevere I'll win? I'll get the response I want?'

Briony eyed him scornfully. 'If you mean that you'll win Thornton Hall then the answer is no. Damn you, Nicholas, you'll never win. This house is mine and it's staying that way.' Her anger was bubbling over. He was a cunning, conniving man, using his sexuality to get his hands on the property, and if she wasn't careful she would be in danger of succumbing, falling prey to his undeniable sexuality, and losing her claim to the house in the bargain.

There was no doubt in her mind that if they became lovers, if she let herself fall under his spell, then it wouldn't be long before he got his name on the deeds as well, and from then on, if their relationship foundered, he would fight for complete possession. She headed for the stairs and was halfway up when he spoke again.

'I have something to tell you about my father.'

Briony was instantly alert, turning and looking at him and coming down a couple of steps.

'I was right about Normac being formed by the Camerons. In fact the whole affair, right from the moment orders stopped coming in, was a set-up.'

'Have you proof?' asked Briony with a frown. It seemed a rather sweeping statement.

'What does Normac spell backwards?'

She thought for a moment. 'Camron, but—but that's——'

'That's just it,' he cut in fiercely. 'It's so corny, so unlikely, and yet it's the truth. I was playing around with the name Normac in my mind today and it suddenly struck me that it was Cameron minus the e. They actually flaunted their name at my father and he never knew.'

'It could still be coincidence,' said Briony. 'Maybe you're jumping to conclusions.'

'I have proof all right,' he told her grimly. 'All of the directors of Normac are members of the Cameron family one way or another. They chose their people carefully.'

'You're sure about this?'

'It's a fact, I've double-checked. Even the company that took all the orders off my father in the first place was set up by the Camerons.' He was violently angry, on his high horse because of the foul deeds that had ruined James Thornton.

'And that's why I lost my job as well? The Camerons wanted *me* out?'

Nicholas inclined his head. 'It was all a well-organised plot.'

'I cannot believe that anyone would go to all these lengths because of some silly feud,' she said.

'It was because *I* took their daughter off them and, what was worse, didn't bring her happiness. She's lost to them now and they blame me.'

'But it's not your fault.'

'Try telling them that. But I shall get my own back even if it takes me the rest of my life. It's the least I can do for my father.'

'Don't you think you ought to let sleeping dogs lie?' she asked softly. 'It's done, it's finished with; why cause fresh anger?'

He looked at her as though she were a complete idiot. 'You really think I'd let them ruin us and do nothing about it? The business is gone; the house would have been gone if I hadn't turned up when I did. I'm actually surprised they haven't tried to buy it themselves—unless they're waiting until it reaches a rock-bottom price. Oh, no, Briony, I'm most certainly not sitting back and doing nothing. It's my inheritance we're talking about here.'

'And that's what's important, isn't it?' she asked scathingly. '*Your* inheritance. Thornton Hall. Not so much the business, but this house, and it doesn't matter who you hurt in the process—you just want it for yourself.'

His breath came out in an impatient hiss. 'Of course it damn well isn't just Thornton Hall. It's justice we're talking about. The family name, the family honour, nothing else.'

Briony did not entirely believe him. It was this house that mattered and he was going to get his hands on it by fair means or foul.

CHAPTER NINE

WHEN Paul arrived to pick her up Briony was ready and waiting, and she ran out to his car before he could come to the door. She did not want a further confrontation with Nicholas.

She could not help thinking that it was a whole lot different sitting beside Paul. There was no choking air, no difficulty in breathing—nothing, in fact. It was like being with a platonic friend.

Paul had never, not even in the early days of their relationship, set her body on fire—not in the way Nicholas did. Nevertheless, they had a comfortable relationship, and she had never craved anything different. If Nicholas hadn't turned up she would have eventually married Paul and probably been very happy. She would not have known what she was missing. But now she did, and it made a difference, and she knew that it was time to put an end to things.

The question was, how? She did not want to hurt Paul by bluntly saying that it was all over, that she did not love him any more. He would immediately think it was because she preferred Nicholas to him, and that wasn't true. Maybe she was attracted to Nicholas physically, but that didn't mean to say that she loved the guy. Oh, no, he was the last man in the world with whom she would want a committed relationship.

Paul took her to his favourite restaurant in a neighbouring town and nothing was said about Nicholas until they were settled and piping hot tomato soup had been served. Then he said, 'I don't like that man living with you. Surely you could have come to some other arrangement?' There was resentment in his tone and a hurt expression on his face, almost as though he were blaming her for the whole thing.

'Such as what?' It took an effort for Briony to keep her tone level. How could he possibly think that it was her fault?

'I don't know,' he said frowningly, 'but to actually let him move in... It's tantamount to saying that he has some right to the house.'

Briony shot him a disgusted glance. 'It wasn't my choice.'

'So why didn't you stop him?'

'Nicholas Grant is like a bulldozer,' she retorted fiercely. 'If you hadn't been away it might have been different. He's not the type of guy a girl can handle on her own.'

'I'd certainly have made sure he didn't move in,' he claimed.

Briony privately wondered whether he would have been able to. Last night he hadn't been particularly aggressive towards Nicholas, not as much as she would have liked. Paul usually took the easy way out of things. He did not like arguments and fights.

'He also had the blessing of the solicitor,' she informed him, 'or so he said. They're working on the premise that there is a second will somewhere and he has as much right to live there as I do.'

'But that's diabolical,' grated Paul. 'Have you looked for the will?'

'Of course I have—I've searched everywhere. There are still a few more bookshelves to hunt through, just in case James slipped it inside or between one of the books, but otherwise there's no sign of it.'

Paul shook his head, as though all this was beyond him. 'Do you think it exists, or do you think this guy is making it up?'

Briony shrugged as she took another mouthful of her soup. 'The letter he showed me from his father seemed genuine enough, but I can't believe that James would never have said anything.'

'It's certainly a very peculiar set-up and I want you to promise me, Briony, that you won't let him touch you again. I realise he's a very attractive guy, but you must be strong. Don't forget—he's after only one thing and that is Thornton Hall.'

She squirmed inside and wondered if her guilt showed on her face. How could she promise when it was already too late? No matter how often she vowed to herself not to let Nicholas get through to her, she always lost. She was putty in his hands and, although he had stopped last night when she asked him, there would inevitably come a time when he would take no notice of her protests. And would she want him to?

'Briony?'

She realised he was still waiting for her answer and with a thumping heart she said, 'Of course I promise, Paul.'

'I think we ought to set a date for our wedding.'

This was ironic after what she had said to Nicholas and her eyes widened, her heart beating even more violently. She could see why he was suggesting it—he was frightened of losing her to this other man. While there had been no opposition he had been perfectly content to sit back and do nothing. Now, all of a sudden, he saw his future slipping away from him.

Although she knew now would be the ideal time to tell Paul that she wanted to end their relationship, she somehow could not bring herself to hurt him. It would be best to wind things down slowly so that when the crunch came he would not be so upset.

'I think we should wait until the matter of the house has been sorted.' Even to her own ears her voice sounded panic-stricken. 'I mean, we've waited six years—a few more months won't make any difference, surely? I can't possibly plan a wedding with all this worry about the house hanging over me.'

He looked at her with a suspicious frown creasing his brow. 'You're sure that's all it is?'

'Of course I'm sure.'

'It's not because of that man—Nicholas Grant Thornton, or whatever his name is?'

Briony shook her head. 'I've told you—he means nothing to me. I dislike him intensely.'

'And that kiss—it meant nothing either?'

'He's a more demonstrative person than you,' she explained wryly. 'It's natural to him to kiss someone goodnight, even the slightest of acquaintances. There was nothing in it.'

'His daughter hinted that she had seen you kissing before.'

Briony silently cursed Josephine and her big mouth. What had the girl hoped to gain? Unless she thought Paul would lay into her father and insist that he kept his hands off her? It would have been nice for Paul to defend her in that way but she was beginning to realise more and more that he wasn't much of a man, and she wondered why she had stuck him all these years.

'I've told you,' she said quietly. 'It's just the way he is.'

'You didn't have to let him kiss you,' he grumbled.

Briony drew in a deep, ragged sigh. 'I didn't seem to have much choice.'

'You mean you didn't want to stop him.' Paul shook his head, his eyes worried. 'I think there's more to this than you're telling me, but for the moment I'm prepared to give you the benefit of the doubt.'

When he took her home it was only half-past nine. He did not come in because he was anxious to get back to his mother, who apparently wasn't well, and his kiss was sweet, gentle and friendly. It would never set her pulses racing and she knew, finally, that it was not enough. Nicholas was right when he said she would be bored out of her mind if she married Paul. It would be a routine, humdrum existence, which he seemed to thrive on, but which would drive her crazy—and it was all thanks to Nicholas that she had found this out! How she hated having to thank this man for anything.

'Well, my, my, what an early bird you are, and what a feeble little kiss it was your boyfriend gave you.'

Briony's eyes met Nicholas's as she entered the house, and his jeering words made her hackles rise. 'How dare you spy on us?' she cried. 'What a mean, despicable thing to do.'

'I just happened to be looking out of the window,' he announced carelessly. 'What a wonderful invention the security light is. I saw everything in finest detail.'

'You swine!' Briony took a swing at him, but he caught her wrist easily and grinned into her face.

'Tell me what sort of an evening you had.'

'It's no business of yours,' she rasped, trying her hardest to wrench free, feeling immediately his intoxicating headiness. It swirled around her like a drug and made her lose all sense of what was right and what was wrong.

His dark eyes penetrated hers. 'I think it's very much my business.' There was a low, soft growl to his voice which sent shivers shuddering down her spine. 'Did you tell him that it's all over between you?' He had her two hands imprisoned now, holding them down at her side, their bodies touching.

Briony's adrenalin had never run so high and she closed her eyes, refusing to look at him, to see his disturbing sexuality. 'No, I didn't,' she said softly.

'Did you—propose marriage?'

She felt the sudden tensing in him. 'We talked about it, yes,' she agreed.

He let her go with an angry gesture. 'How could you, Briony? How could you? God, can't you see that he's entirely the wrong person for you? What are you trying to do—ruin your whole life?'

'I think I know what I'm doing,' she told him coldly, taking the opportunity to step away from him.

He shook his head in exasperation. 'I'm not so sure that you do. Despite the short time we've known each other, I think I can safely claim that your feelings for me are much stronger. I only saw Paul for a few minutes, damn it, but there were no vibes between you, no crackling electricity, which is how it should be between two people contemplating marriage; there was nothing. How can you stand there and say that you're going to marry the guy?'

'It strikes me that you're getting all worked up over nothing,' Briony tossed back. 'What's it to you what I do? Why should you care whether I make a mess of my life or not?'

'Because I genuinely care about you.'

She looked at him with eyes full of scepticism, wishing she could believe him, but knowing it was all a pack of lies. 'That's rich; all you care about is this house. I am merely a means to an end. Don't try to deny it.'

Amazingly he looked hurt. 'Don't you love me even a little?'

Her eyes widened. 'What a crazy question. Are you out of your mind? Whatever I feel, it certainly isn't love. You're the last person in the world I'd fall in love with.'

'So it's lust you feel when you respond to me?'

'Lust suggests an over-sexed person,' she retorted sharply, 'and that's certainly not me.'

Nicholas touched his hands to her shoulders. 'Then what is it that you feel?' he asked softly.

Briony looked into the smouldering depths of his eyes and how she contained herself she did not know; how she kept her eyes on his and did not lift herself up on tiptoe to press her lips against his was a miracle. She felt charged with electric impulses and hated herself for being so weak. She must remember that he was her enemy and only after the house.

'I know you want to kiss me, Briony.' His voice was deep and low and sent even more shivers through her body. 'So why torture yourself? Why tell yourself that you must remain true to Paul? You deserve better.'

'Better being you?' Her tone was harsh and critical, but nevertheless her body flooded with warmth and she ached in every limb to be possessed by this man. He was really getting through to her and the longer he lived in this house the worse it would be.

His hands slid up her back, caressing, persuading, shattering every ounce of self-control. He took hold of her face between his palms and looked down into the luminous depths of her eyes and suddenly she was in her own little cocoon of time. No one else existed besides this man. They could have been anywhere—anywhere in the world—and it would have been the same. Only he mattered.

'You could do worse than me, Briony.' His tone was as eloquent as his hands. He triggered off such sensations that no inch of her body was free of him. Her breathing deepened and she knew she ought to say something, ought to stop him, but she had no control. It was gone, all gone under this man's spell.

A gentle finger traced the outline of her face, the soft curve of her cheek, the fine arch of her brows, finally assaulting her parted lips.

Without even realising what she was doing, Briony touched the tip of her tongue to his finger, feeling the slight roughness of his skin, tasting his essential maleness, her body moving into him, swaying gently, the headiness of the moment almost spinning her into space.

He gave a faint groan and his mouth swooped down to capture hers, and if Briony thought of Paul it was only fleetingly. This was what she wanted: these mind-drugging kisses, the incredible sensations, the roaring need. Her throat arched as she returned his kiss, and she felt herself drowning in the wash of her desire.

His kiss deepened when he met no resistance, his tongue touching hers, probing the inner recesses of her mouth, filling her with such sweet ecstasy that it was almost like a pain within her breast.

He stopped only when they were both gasping for air, but he did not let her go; he pulled her head into his shoulder, stroking her hair, murmuring soft, unintelligible words. He was so gentle that it was incredible, so caring, so utterly unlike the ruthless man who had first walked into her life. She did not want to move, she did not want this magic moment to end; on the other hand she was afraid of where it might lead.

She was totally surprised when he let her go; she felt bereft, puzzled, completely disorientated. This was not what she had anticipated; she had expected another replay of last night, and if the truth were known she would have had difficulty in stopping him this time, wouldn't even have wanted to.

'I need a drink,' he said gruffly. 'Will you join me?'

Briony knew she ought to refuse, ought to go up to her room and put as much distance between them as possible, but somehow she found herself agreeing, and two hours later they were still sitting together, talking inconsequentially about all manner of things.

He had not tried to kiss her again; in fact he had not touched her. On the other hand he had not taken his eyes off her. They sat in separate chairs facing each other and Briony felt on fire, felt an intense awareness, an aching need. She had no defence against him at all.

He was showing her yet another side to him: a charming companion, a good talker, a good listener, intelligent, friendly, funny—everything you could ever want in a man. The trouble was that she could not forget that he was after the house, that all this was pretence, a means to an end.

Eventually she yawned and stretched. 'I think I'll go to bed.'

'Me too,' he agreed, rising at the same time.

He put the lights out and they climbed the stairs together. Outside her door he stopped and Briony thought, this is it, this is where I have to start fighting him off. To her surprise all he did was press a kiss to her brow, saying softly, 'Goodnight, honey, sweet dreams.' And then he carried on along the corridor to his own room.

Briony was stunned. She went inside and sat on the edge of the bed. She could not understand him. This wasn't what she had expected at all. Was it all part of some ingenious plot? Was he deliberately trying to torment her? Playing with her emotions so that the next time he wanted to make love to her she would be ready for him? She did not know; she could not make him out. All she knew was that he was the most sexually exciting man she had ever met.

As she lay in bed later Briony could not help contrasting the two parts of the evening, and she knew which half she had enjoyed most. It was very wrong and very dangerous, but she had no control. It was no good telling herself to ignore Nicholas, to maintain a distance between them, because it wouldn't work. He had already insinuated himself into her mind, her thoughts, her emotions. Every part of her recognised him, was tormented by him, and she did not know what to do about it.

A few more days passed in similar vein—no kissing, no touching, simply eye contact and endless conversations. For the life of her Briony could never remember what they talked about; she was aware only of Nicholas and the immense hold he had over her. When he asked when she was going to see Paul again she suddenly realised that he had not been in touch since Tuesday.

'I usually only see him at weekends,' she said. 'He works most evenings.'

'Doesn't he even telephone?'

'It all depends how busy he is,' excused Briony.

Nicholas shook his head in disgust. 'And you're going to marry such a thoughtless, pathetic little character?'

Immediately she was on the defensive. 'Paul isn't like that at all; it's just unfortunate that his job means him working during the evenings.'

'And what sort of a married life would it mean for you?'

Briony eyed him coldly. 'It earns him a respectable living; that's the important thing.'

'And you wouldn't mind being on your own night after night?'

'I've been used to it since my mother died. It's no great problem.'

'I can't see why Holman didn't move in with you; it would have helped with the expenses, and you might not have felt it necessary to sell. Didn't he ever suggest it?'

'Paul looks after his mother.' Briony's eyes began to spark with anger. She hated it when he asked all these questions, when he insisted on belittling Paul.

Nicholas snorted. 'So what will happen to her when you do get married? Surely you're not planning to move in with her?' He looked positively disgusted at the thought.

'Of course not.' But there was no conviction in her voice. She and Paul had never actually discussed where they would live, but she knew he would find it very difficult to break away. She supposed she ought to ask herself why they had not talked about it. This was yet another reason why she ought to give Paul up. They had drifted on for far too long without making any positive decisions.

'So you were planning to buy a nice house somewhere with the proceeds from the sale of this place?' There was a gruffness to his tone and a hardness to his eyes. He was once again the cold, ruthless stranger, and every single warm feeling Briony had felt drained out of her.

'Naturally.' What she did not tell him was that she and Paul had never discussed it, that the house would be for herself alone. 'And as a matter of fact I've decided that I am still going to sell if a buyer comes along,' she added belligerently.

Nicholas gave a bellow of anger. 'You cannot do that; things have changed now. I have as much right to this house as you.'

'Only if the will is found.'

His eyes narrowed suspiciously. 'You seem pretty sure that it won't be. Perhaps you know something that I don't? Perhaps you've actually found it and destroyed it?' He took her shoulders, fingers biting, hurting— nothing at all like his sensual caresses, which had stayed with her for so long. 'Tell me, Briony.' He shook her violently. 'Tell me what you've done with it.'

'You're hurting me,' she retorted.

'Then give me your answer,' he growled, making no attempt to lessen his grip.

'Damn you, Nicholas, I've found no will.' Her eyes were as blazingly furious as his. 'Do you really think I'd stoop so low as to destroy it if I had?'

'I'd like to think not, but who knows how you'd behave in exceptional circumstances?' He finally relaxed his fingers, but he did not let her go; instead he bowed his head and kissed her fiercely.

Briony twisted away. 'You're disgusting,' she spat.

'I have tickets for the theatre tomorrow night; I'd like you to join me.'

His complete about-turn baffled her and she shook her head wildly. 'I don't understand you; one minute you're accusing me of some vile deed, the next you want to take me out.'

'Will you come?' There was still a glittering light in his eyes, but he was relaxed now, his thumbs hooked into his belt in his usual easy stance.

'No,' she told him positively. 'I always see Paul on a Saturday night.'

'But you've just said you haven't heard from him all week.'

'It makes no difference; Saturday night is our night, always.'

He pursed his lips. 'It would be a pity to waste the tickets.'

'It's a pity you bought them without asking me first. Take your daughter.' She was still angry with him, wouldn't even have agreed if she wasn't going out. He really did have two sides to his character. She wondered when his birthday was, whether he was a Gemini, whether his mercurial changes of mood depended solely upon his star sign?

'Jojo doesn't like straight plays. She prefers pop concerts,' he told her.

'Then it's your bad luck if the tickets are wasted. Go by yourself, find another woman, do what the hell you like; just don't expect me to come with you.'

It was much later in the evening when the telephone rang; in fact Briony was thinking about going to bed. The last two hours had been extremely uncomfortable. They had both continued to sit in the living-room, she with a magazine open on her lap, Nicholas watching a programme on the TV. But she could not concentrate; she was too aware of Nicholas. Angry though she was with him, the old feelings had returned, torturing her, unsettling her, making her hate herself for being so weak.

She answered the telephone in the kitchen, well away from Nicholas's listening ears. She had a feeling it would be Paul, even though it was much later than he usually rang.

She was right. 'Hello, Briony,' he said. 'I'm sorry I haven't phoned you before. Mother's not at all well, I'm afraid.'

'Oh, dear, what's wrong?' she asked sympathetically.

'I'm not really sure, but she's in bed and needs my constant attention.'

'Have you called in the doctor?'

'Mother won't let me. I'm afraid I won't be able to see you tomorrow night; I must look after her.'

'I'll come over there if you like,' said Briony at once. If Nicholas knew she had no excuse to go out he would insist on her accompanying him to the theatre, and although she knew she would enjoy the play she was worried because they were spending so much time together.

'She doesn't want visitors, I'm afraid, Briony. I'm sorry—I hate having to do this, especially with that man sharing your house. How are things going?'

Briony explained that there was no sign of the will yet, not telling him that she had spent every minute she was at home with Nicholas and that she had not had chance to look.

'I'm sure James's solicitor will sort it all out when he returns,' he said. 'Just be careful until then. I told Mother about us hoping to get married in the not too distant future.'

'What did she say?' asked Briony sharply.

'Not a lot, though I'm sure she was expecting it.'

Exactly, thought Briony, and her illness now was a direct reaction to it. Mrs Holman had very convenient illnesses. There would never be a right time for Paul to get married, always his mother would need him. Why couldn't he see that?

'I'll ring you on Sunday,' he went on. 'If Mother's better by then perhaps we can go for a drive.'

'Yes, that would be nice,' she answered weakly. 'Give her my best wishes.'

She put the receiver down and as she turned around Nicholas was standing behind her.

'So you're not seeing him tomorrow night.' There was a delighted smile on his face. 'That means you'll be able to come out with me after all.'

'You were listening!' she accused. 'How low can you get?'

'I gather Paul's mother's not well? How inconvenient for you two, but convenient for me. You have no reason now not to take up my offer.'

'Except that I don't want to go to the theatre with you.'

He frowned faintly. 'Why not?'

'I think we're seeing too much of each other,' she answered coolly. 'The original idea, when you took up residence here, was to have our own separate rooms. Jo's abided by that, but you haven't, and I'm beginning to resent the way you're imposing your time upon mine.'

Black brows rose. 'I got the impression that you were beginning to accept me, to enjoy my company. Am I wrong?'

Briony clamped her lips and did not answer for a second or two. 'I suppose I was, but that's what is wrong. You're my enemy, you're trying to force me out of my home; I don't want to like you.'

'So it's yourself you're fighting, not me?' A hint of a smile curved the fullness of his lips and he stepped forward to take her into his arms, but Briony backed away.

'Don't touch me,' she spat.

This time he gave a roar of laughter. 'That is rich, after the way you've been responding to me all week. I could have taken you any second I wanted, Briony, and you know it.'

Briony shrugged. 'That was then, this is now; it's different.'

'What's different?'

'I've come to my senses. I hate you.'

Once more he laughed. 'I love feisty ladies. Come to the theatre with me and I promise to keep my hands off you all night.'

'No.'

'Please, pretty please.' He got down on his knees and put his hands together and he looked so ludicrous that Briony burst out laughing.

'OK, you win, but no going back on your word. It's hands off all evening or I'll walk out on you.'

CHAPTER TEN

BRIONY dressed carefully for her evening at the theatre in a fine woollen blue dress, its full skirt and fitted bodice emphasising her curves. It was not often she wore something so figure-hugging, but she knew that it suited her, and Nicholas's appraising glance when she came downstairs spoke volumes.

The play was an excellent, tense drama, and she was so engrossed that she was able to forget, to a certain degree, Nicholas sitting beside her. Not altogether, of course; she could never do that. Whether her mood was anger, resentment or whatever, she was always aware of him, always; but the fact that he too was intent on the scenes unfolding on the stage helped a lot.

They had drinks in the interval and still he was as good as his word. He did not touch her or make any undue moves or suggestions; Briony actually began to relax and enjoy herself until—when the play ended—he declared that he had a table booked at a nearby restaurant. She looked at him sharply and incredulously. 'This isn't part of the plan at all.' She had counted on going straight home, avoiding any sort of prolonged intimacy with him.

'If you'd known you'd have refused to come out with me.' His smile said he knew her only too well. 'Tonight you are mine; it would be wrong not to make the most of it.' In his dark grey suit, white silk shirt and burgundy tie he was devastatingly handsome. No one could ever say that Nicholas did not dress well; whether it was casual wear or something more formal he always looked exactly right, but there was something else about him—an air of power, of supreme confidence, of being master of his own destiny.

'I am not yours,' she corrected smartly, 'nor will I ever be.' Not in the true sense of the word. She might be his for brief moments in time, times when she lost her senses, times when sensuality seemed all that mattered, but not always, not by a long chalk.

His hand was on her elbow as he led her from the auditorium. 'Haven't you yet realised that what I want I usually get?' he muttered, and there was laughter in his voice.

'Maybe you usually do,' she agreed, 'but not this time.'

'I thrive on challenges,' he reminded her, his mouth close to her ear, warm, husky and exciting.

'You mean you enjoy the thrill of the pursuit?' she parried.

'Among other things,' he answered darkly.

Outside he hailed and got a taxi while others were still waiting and within minutes they were at his chosen restaurant. Not a place Briony had been to before, being much more expensive than anything Paul could afford. It was thickly carpeted, elegantly furnished in deep blue, pink and gold. Her coat was whisked away, drinks were ordered, they were seated in deep, comfortable chairs, and leather-bound menus were placed in front of them.

Soft, non-intrusive music played, and Briony felt that she had entered a different world. James had sometimes asked her to join him and Patricia when they dined out and always it had been somewhere nice, but this was different: this was her and Nicholas, and the atmosphere was charged. It was not only the place, it was the company.

When they were shown to their table Briony was astonished to see beside it a bottle of champagne sitting in a silver bucket filled with ice. 'What are we celebrating?' she asked with a faint frown.

'Whatever you wish to celebrate,' he answered enigmatically.

A crisp pink napkin was draped on her lap, their chosen starters placed in front of them. 'I wish you wouldn't do things like this,' said Briony, tasting her chicken mousse dressed in tarragon mayonnaise with ham. It was probably very delicious, but at this moment in time all she could think of was that she was here under duress.

'Like what?' Nicholas asked.

'Bring me out like this. It's unnecessary and unwanted.' She knew she sounded ungrateful, but it was all beyond anything that was needed from him.

'Now there's gratitude,' he quipped, completely unperturbed by her words. 'If I were you, Briony, I'd sit back and enjoy yourself; it has to be far better than spending an evening alone.'

She lifted her shoulders in a defenceless little shrug. 'Obviously, but I don't know what you're hoping to gain from it.'

'Your friendship?' he suggested, one eyebrow raised.

'Or Thornton Hall?' she parried coolly.

Eyes narrowed. 'Dammit, Briony,' he growled, 'do you have to spoil everything? Can't we forget the house just for tonight?'

'When it's the most important thing in your life?' she tossed back. 'I bet you never forget it. I bet you never forget that I own what you want most in this world. You can pretend all you like, Nicholas; I know exactly what's at the back of your mind.'

A flash of anger shot through his eyes, controlled almost instantly, but it was not so easy for him to check the muscle that jerked in his jaw. 'This is neither the time nor the place to indulge in arguments of this kind,' he told her evenly. 'My plan was to make tonight a pleasurable occasion.'

'Pleasurable for whom?' she enquired, her tone still rejecting him.

'Both of us, hopefully. Hell, Briony, this is most unfair.'

'I didn't want to come; I only reluctantly agreed to the theatre, and then to find this...' She waved a disparaging hand towards the champagne. 'It makes me suspicious, to say the least.'

'Suspicious?' he echoed, black brows drawing together in a furious frown.

'It's entirely uncalled for.'

'You're being unreasonable, Briony.'

'Am I? I don't think so. I can only presume that you thought you'd have something to celebrate tonight. My capitulation, perhaps?' She eyed him stonily. 'I hate to disappoint you but you've wasted your money. You're no nearer to winning me over than you were in the beginning.'

They were lies, all lies, but she had to keep up the pretence, otherwise she would once more give way to the very real sensations that ran deep inside her, and that would be disastrous.

'You've got me all wrong; my intentions are perfectly honourable,' he assured her, but the muscle still jerked and his eyes were cold. 'I merely want you to enjoy yourself. Your life hasn't been easy this past year; you deserve to be spoilt a little.'

Briony eyed him doubtfully and shook her head. 'You don't really expect me to believe that's all you have in mind, not after what we've gone through?'

'You're being unnecessarily hard on me.' He reached out across the table and touched her hand and Briony's first instinct was to snatch away, but she didn't. Her biggest mistake, however, was letting her eyes meet his. Instantly she felt herself drowning, sinking into a quagmire of sensations and emotions from which she knew there would be no escape unless she kept a tight rein on them.

'Believe me, Briony,' he went on, 'all I want tonight is the pleasure of your company, nothing more, nothing less. Why can't we call a truce? Let's pretend we've just met, that there are no differences between us whatsoever.'

Briony gave an inward groan. She had already weighed up such a situation. With no threat of losing her home, only the pleasure this man could give her, she would have no hang-ups whatsoever. She would give herself to him freely and openly, let him see how much she cared, what she felt. But she dared not do this, not in the circumstances. He would use it against her. She must, at all costs, maintain a certain distance between them.

'So long as you still ask nothing of me,' she agreed eventually, reluctantly. It was the only answer she could give him. It didn't mean a lot, because she knew he would never be able to forget who she was.

'It's a deal,' he said with a pleased smile, his hand tightening fractionally on hers before letting her go.

The waiter came at a signal from Nicholas and poured champagne into their glasses. 'To us,' he said softly when the man had gone. 'To friendship.'

'Friendship,' she agreed, taking a sip and wrinkling her nose as the bubbles tickled it.

They had reached their main course when Briony caught the eye of a man at one of the other tables. It was the very same colleague of Paul's who had seen them together in the Red Lion. 'I don't believe this,' she muttered, half to herself.

'What's wrong?' asked Nicholas at once.

'I've just seen a friend of Paul's.'

'And you're afraid he'll tell him you've been out with another man?' There was mockery in his tone and it was evident he did not care one little bit.

'I did assure Paul that you meant nothing to me,' she flashed, annoyed by his disregard for her feelings.

'You probably told him you hated my guts as well?' Still the infuriating smile softened the harsh angles of his face.

'More or less.'

'So I wonder what he'll make of us being out together now? It makes a mockery of your plans to get married, doesn't it?'

'It changes nothing,' she snapped.

'That might not be what Paul thinks.'

'And you'd like him to call it all off, wouldn't you?' she asked hostilely. 'Hell, I knew tonight was a mistake. How can we be friends?'

'All we have to do is forget Paul and concentrate on ourselves,' he said softly.

Briony shook her head, her eyes flashing her impatience. 'How can I forget him when there's a guy who knows him well over there watching every move we make? I think we should leave.'

'And let him see that you're bothered? It would be like shutting the stable door after the horse has bolted. Rise above it, Briony.'

He was right; it was too late. All she could hope for was that her face had not given anything away. It was very unfortunate that this man had seen her twice with Nicholas because he would now draw his own conclusions, and she knew without a doubt that they would not be in her favour.

It was difficult to pretend he was not there, and although they drank the champagne and chatted and laughed she was uneasy. She could feel herself being watched and condemned, and if the man hadn't told Paul about the previous occasion he had seen them together she was confident he would now.

In the circumstances it should not matter—one day their relationship would end anyway—but she did not want it to be like this; she wanted to let Paul down gently. After six years she felt she owed him something.

It was a relief when their coffee-cups were empty and they were finally ready to leave. The unfortunate part was that they had to walk past the table where Paul's colleague was sitting openly and interestedly watching them.

Briony gave him a faint smile, knowing that to pretend she had not seen him would compound her guilt even further. Nicholas, who had not seen the man until now, nodded pleasantly as well, thus drawing even more attention to himself, and Briony could have willingly kicked his shins.

Nevertheless she decided to say nothing, letting Nicholas help her into the taxi, sitting in the corner well away from him, her hands clutching her bag on her lap, putting up a defensive wall around her.

'Stop worrying,' ordered Nicholas, and when she turned her head he was watching her. It was too dark to read the true expression in his eyes, but she sensed compassion and this surprised her—it was something she did not normally associate with him. 'If Paul truly loves you he'll understand. Why shouldn't you go out if he stands you up? Why should you sit and wait? I think you've done enough of that over the years. After all, he doesn't own you—yet.'

It was his emphasis on the final word that made Briony say sharply, 'But my loyalties lie with him all the same. I wish you hadn't taken me there tonight.'

'What's done is done,' he growled, impatience creeping into his voice. 'Just forget the guy, Briony. Dammit, this was supposed to be a special evening, one where we got to know each other better, where all our differences and worries were put behind us.'

Briony shrugged. 'I can't help the way I am. I do have a conscience, you know.'

'And that conscience will make you tell Paul about tonight—before his friend does?' There was disgust in his tone this time. 'On the other hand,' he went on, suddenly grinning, 'it might do me a favour.'

Briony looked at him suspiciously, frowningly.

'Without Paul in the background you'll be able to give free rein to your emotions without fear of feeling guilty.' He was confident now, sliding across the seat towards her. 'You'll have no reason for second thoughts, for feeling that you're letting him down.' His hard, muscled thigh was against hers, triggering a chain of sensations so strong that Briony found it difficult to breathe.

She tried to edge away, but there was nowhere to go, and she took defence in anger. 'In other words, it gives you a clear field, is that what you're saying?' It was precisely the thoughts that had rushed through her own mind, but she hated it when he made assumptions like this. She hated him knowing how she felt.

'I don't have to tell you again that I think you'd be making a big mistake if you did marry Paul. As for me having a clear field, well, I think there are still a lot of obstacles to climb.'

'You're dead right, there are,' snapped Briony. 'Insurmountable ones.'

'Oh, no. Believe me, I shall get what I want in the end.'

Briony glared at him from her prison in the corner. His confidence was staggering, and she knew exactly what he meant. He wasn't talking about her, he was talking about Thornton Hall. She was merely a means to an end; and to stop him getting his hands on the house meant stopping him getting his hands on her!

'Will you move away from me?' she spat through gritted teeth.

'Afraid of yourself, Briony?' he taunted.

'I'm afraid of nothing,' she tossed back scornfully. 'I just don't happen to like being suffocated.'

He did not move; instead he inched even closer, his hand coming up to her face, turning her head so that she was compelled to look into the powerful depths of his eyes. 'If I suffocate you, Briony, I apologise, but somehow I don't think that's the truth. 'You're using it as an excuse to hide behind, anything rather than admit that you're attracted to me.'

His face loomed close and before she could speak, before she could defend herself, his mouth came down upon hers. It was no bruising, demanding kiss; it was gentle and persuasive instead, asking, persuading, encouraging.

Briony closed her eyes and her head fell back against the seat. She fought to remain passive but as the seconds ticked away she could keep up the effort no longer. Even now the blood was rushing and tingling through her veins, warming her skin, exciting her pulses. It was an inevitable reaction no matter how she fought, especially coming on top of the champagne and brandy, which had already made her feel light-headed.

She really had no idea how long the kiss lasted; she was aware of nothing until Nicholas drew away from her and the taxi pulled up outside the Hall. He helped her out, quickly paid the driver, and with his arm about her waist they walked into the house.

It could have all led to something more than Briony wanted at this stage if they hadn't been disrupted by an ear-piercing shriek from upstairs, followed by raucous laughter—male laughter!

'What the hell?' Nicholas let Briony go instantly and bounded up the stairs three at a time. Briony followed, but before she had even reached the top a red-faced youth was being propelled out of the house by the back of his collar. 'Hell, I wasn't doing anything wrong,' he protested.

'That's not what it looked like to me,' growled Nicholas. 'Get out and stay out; you're not welcome here.' The instant the door shut behind the lad he headed back up the stairs. '*Josephine*, I want a word with you.'

It was the first time Briony had ever heard him call his daughter by her full name. Lord, he was angry, but she couldn't blame him. Goodness knew what they'd been up to all evening.

Although she would have liked to know the outcome, Briony took the opportunity to go to her room. She was, in actual fact, glad of the respite. Tomorrow would be another trying day. If Paul phoned and suggested they went for a drive she would have to tell him about her evening out, and if he didn't she would have Nicholas to face again. Either way she couldn't win.

Thankfully Richard Brent would be returning on Monday, she thought as she climbed into bed. How she wished she could say that the house had been thoroughly searched and no will found. The trouble was she'd had no time to look—Nicholas made sure of that—although she had no doubt that when she was at work he himself searched every nook and cranny.

The more she thought about the will, the more she felt that it did not exist. In the twelve-month period after James and her mother died she had gone through the house from top to bottom. Top to bottom! It suddenly occurred to her that she had not looked in the attic; in fact she had never, ever been up there. But would James put something so important in the attic? No, she dismissed the thought; it was ridiculous, of course he wouldn't.

However, the thought persisted, and she knew that she would not rest until she looked. She would have liked to do it when she had the house to herself, but since

Nicholas only seemed to go out when she was at work
that was an impossibility. They would have to do it
together. Her last thoughts as she fell asleep were that
she would suggest it tomorrow.

But on Sunday morning Paul telephoned and said that
his mother was slightly better and perhaps they could
go out and maybe have lunch somewhere. 'I don't want
to leave her all day, you understand, but for two or three
hours she'll be all right.'

Nicholas, as usual, had listened unashamedly to her
conversation. 'Will this morning be the big confession
job?'

There was derision in his tone, and Briony looked at
him scornfully. 'What I do or don't do is no business
of yours.'

Black brows rose. 'I happen to think it's very much
my business. You can't argue with the fact that the more
we see of each other the closer we're becoming. It's very
unfortunate that we always seem to be interrupted, but
nevertheless there is definitely something growing between us.'

He was right, so right, but she shook her head regardless. 'You're talking nonsense. What we have is
animal attraction, nothing upon which to build a relationship. I actually cannot understand how I react the
way I do when I despise you so much.'

He perched himself on one of the kitchen stools.
'Perhaps we should analyse why you despise me—or
think you do?'

Briony had just finished clearing away after her
breakfast. His daughter was still asleep, or else sulking
after her telling-off last night. 'Believe me, I don't think
it, I know it,' she returned sharply. 'And why do I despise you? Because of the way you walked into this house
and tried to take over, because of the way you're pushing
yourself into my life, because the only reason you're

showing any interest in me is so that you can get your hands on the house if the will fails to materialise. Is that enough?' She was breathing heavily, her eyes bright, two spots of high colour flaming her cheeks.

He shook his head, his mouth tight at her harshly spoken words. 'I walked into this house, Briony, because as far as I'm concerned it is still my home, and if you had an ounce of compassion in you you wouldn't quibble about us sharing it. As for you and me, well, I'm simply following my natural instincts; there's nothing calculated in what I'm doing.'

'I don't believe you,' she spat. 'I shall never believe you, no matter what you say. You've one target in mind only, and that is this house.'

'And you've only one thing in mind too,' he growled, 'and that is to believe the worst of me. I'm evidently wasting my time trying to get through to you. Go to your man, enjoy your boring little life with him. One thing I do know is that you'll look back on all of this one day and say to yourself, ''Nicholas was right.'''

Briony did not need him to tell her. She knew that if she did marry Paul she would never be happy, but nor would she be happy living with this man—a man she did not trust, whose motives were purely selfish. She closed her eyes. Why was life so difficult all of a sudden?

'You know I'm right, don't you?'

She looked at him coldly and aggressively. 'I've had enough of this conversation; neither one of us is going to win. Excuse me.'

But it was not so easy getting out of the kitchen. He was off the stool in a flash, blocking her exit. 'Why is it, Briony, that whenever you're losing you always run?'

'Does anyone ever win with you?' she demanded, arms akimbo, eyes furious.

'Not if I consider I'm right.'

'Which is probably always,' she thrust savagely. 'I cannot believe you are James's son; you're so unlike him. He would never treat me like this; he was a gentleman. No wonder he washed his hands of you.'

His mouth twisted angrily. 'That remark was uncalled for.'

'I don't think so,' she spat. 'I speak as I find and you're certainly nothing like your father.' She had respected and loved James; she certainly did not respect this man.

'No two individuals are the same; you can't expect me to be like him.'

Briony shook her head wildly. 'This is a crazy conversation and it's getting us nowhere. Would you mind moving and letting me out?'

'So that you can get ready for your date with lover-boy?' he sneered. 'I'd like to lay a bet that you won't be out long. That once he finds out about last night he'll ditch you like a worn-out shoe.'

'How you change your tune,' she snapped. 'You said last night that he'd understand.'

Nicholas's lips twisted derogatively. 'I said that *if he loved you* he'd understand.'

'And you think he doesn't?'

'I'm sure of it, and I think marriage to him would be a total disaster. But it's your life; go ahead and ruin it.'

Finally he stood back and Briony walked past him. She was actually amazed that he let her go without touching her, but the effect on her body as she moved within inches of him was as devastating as if he had actually pulled her into his arms.

She took her time getting ready. She did not want to be forced to talk to Nicholas again so she hung around in her room. She didn't hear Paul's car pull up, did not realise that he was early, and when she finally went downstairs she was horrified to discover that he was talking to Nicholas.

Had Nicholas told him about last night? she wondered, and decided that he hadn't when Paul greeted her with his normal peck on the cheek. 'Are you ready, darling?'

She nodded. 'I didn't know you were here. I'm sorry if I've kept you waiting.'

'Paul and I have been getting to know one another,' Nicholas informed her, and there was something in his eyes that made Briony suspicious. 'I've been allaying his fears about you and me.'

'You have?'

'Indeed I have.'

'Yes,' confirmed Paul.

'And last night I only took her out because she was devastated when you let her down. I'm sure you understand?'

Briony looked sharply from Nicholas to Paul, saw the sudden shock on the younger man's face.

'You took Briony out last night as well?' Paul gasped.

'That's right,' agreed Nicholas, looking extremely pleased with himself. 'Briony was going to tell you— don't worry, there's nothing underhand about it. She was left with nothing to do after you'd telephoned, I had tickets for the theatre; it was a logical arrangement.'

Briony was furious and didn't know how she stopped herself beating her fists against this dark, arrogant man's chest. How dared he drop the news out just like that? God, what was he trying to do? The answer was plain. He was trying to split them up, doing his very best, in fact, and by appearing to be nice about the whole thing he was making sure he did not get the blame.

'You had *two* tickets and no partner?' queried Paul suspiciously, and Briony did not blame him for thinking that the whole thing had been prearranged. She was sure of it herself.

'Oh, I had a partner in mind all right when I bought them, my daughter. But she suddenly decided that she did not want to go. When Briony told me your mother was ill and you wouldn't be seeing her it seemed a natural thing to ask her if she'd like to come. How is your mother, by the way? I trust she's feeling better.'

It was evident Paul did not know whether to be angry or believe the man. But however Paul felt, Briony was angry, and she glared furiously at Nicholas, determined, when they were alone, to give him a piece of her mind.

'My mother is improving, thank you,' Paul said stiffly, and to Briony, 'We'd better go.'

Nicholas accompanied them to the door, almost as though it were *his* house and he was showing them out, fumed Briony. 'Have a good day, you two,' he said pleasantly.

How could they have a good day after the damage he'd done? Her eyes were bright as she glowered at Nicholas over her shoulder.

He was smiling—a triumphant smile—quite confident that she would come back home today declaring that it was all over between her and Paul. But even if it was, she thought, he needn't think that she would turn to him, because she wouldn't, most definitely not—he was the most hateful man she had ever met.

There was a troubled silence in the car and for the first half a mile Paul said nothing. Briony wondered if he was waiting for her to speak, whether she ought to attempt some form of an apology. But what could she say that would help matters? He would never believe that she had gone against her will, and, really, shouldn't she be thankful that Nicholas was precipitating things for her? Except that she hadn't wanted it to happen like this. She did not want to hurt Paul's feelings; she wanted their relationship to wind down slowly and painlessly. She owed him that much at least.

'Why?' The question came at last and there was so much pain in his voice that Briony squirmed inside.

'He can be very persuasive.'

'And you thought it would do no harm?'

Briony nodded and then whispered, 'Yes.'

'You didn't think I'd be hurt?'

She winced. 'I—I thought you'd understand. After all, you had put me off, and after being so long without you——'

'You turned to someone else?'

'No, no, I didn't,' she cried. 'Not in the way you're suggesting.'

'You still maintain that there's nothing between you?'

'Yes, I do,' she breathed faintly.

'That isn't the impression Nicholas Grant gave.'

Briony looked at him sharply. 'What did he say?' Damn Nicholas. What right had he to imply things like this?

'Never mind what he said, but the impression I got was that you and he are becoming a twosome.'

'In his eyes only,' she tossed back furiously. 'I have told him time and time again that I'm not interested. I know what he's like, what he's after. I hate the man.'

'Then why go out with him?'

Why indeed? She had no answer. 'As I said before, it's difficult to refuse. He's the most forceful man I've ever met.'

'If you *really* didn't want to then he wouldn't be able to make you do it. You're forgetting how well I know you, Briony. You're a strong-minded girl.' He pulled the car into the side of the road and stopped. 'It's all over between us, isn't it? You've fallen for this guy even if you won't admit it.'

'I don't know what I feel,' said Briony, shaking her head in confusion, 'and that's the truth.'

'Could it be that you won't admit to these feelings because of—us? If it's because you don't want to hurt me, Briony, then I'd rather know the truth now. It will be a bitter pill to swallow, I must confess, because I love you and always will, but if your feelings have changed then—there's no point in us going on.'

The fact that he was being so reasonable made Briony feel even worse, and she looked at him with both guilt and sadness in her eyes. 'I can honestly say to you that I don't love Nicholas; on the other hand I don't think my feelings for you are as strong as they were. I'm so sorry, Paul. I still think a lot of you, but perhaps not enough to marry you.'

'And it was this man who made you realise that you didn't love me enough? He's shown you a new way of life, a different side of the coin?'

'It isn't that,' she assured him.

'Then what was it that made you change your mind about me?'

She grimaced ruefully. 'I think we were getting stale, Paul. Six years is a long time to just amble along.'

'I wanted to be sure I could offer you a good lifestyle. It's what all these seminars and courses are about. I'm in line for promotion, Briony. I shall be earning considerably more money. It's what I've been aiming for, why I've not suggested marriage earlier.'

She wanted to ask whether it had anything to do with his mother, but that would be unkind. 'You could have told me,' she said instead. 'I think that's something else that went wrong, lack of communication. I never knew what you were thinking or feeling.'

'I thought you were happy enough?'

'I was.'

'Until Nicholas Grant came into your life?'

'He has changed things,' she admitted, 'but I'm not sure whether it's for the better. I could be out of a home if the will is found.'

'Not if you marry the guy.'

'*Paul*!' she exclaimed, aghast. 'That is not going to happen, no way.'

'It's not what he told me.'

She frowned. 'What do you mean? What did he say?'

'He didn't put it into so many words,' answered Paul. 'In fact he went out of his way to assure me that there was nothing between you, but it was the way that he did it, the way I read between the lines.'

'I'm sure you're wrong,' she said worriedly.

'I don't think so. I think he was very cleverly telling me that I had practically lost you.'

'He had no right,' exclaimed Briony, appalled. 'He had no right at all, and certainly no grounds to make such an assumption. Take me home; I'm going to have this out with him once and for all.'

CHAPTER ELEVEN

PAUL refused to take Briony back to Thornton Hall. 'It would be playing right into Nicholas Grant's hands,' he said. 'Do you really feel nothing for the guy?'

Briony grimaced, but decided honesty was the best policy. 'I would be lying if I said I wasn't attracted to him in one respect, but most of the time I loathe the man. I certainly don't like him enough to want to enter into any sort of relationship.'

'Perhaps it's what he's trying to do to you that you hate?' Paul's face was deadly serious as he looked at her.

Briony shook her head, but nevertheless had the sneaking suspicion that he might have hit on the truth. 'No, it's all of it,' she denied. 'Lord, I wish James had told me about him, I wish he hadn't written that letter. If only he had left something more positive.'

'You don't think there's a second will?'

'Frankly, no.'

'And you're going to fight Nicholas Grant for the house?'

She nodded. 'Most definitely.'

'The problem is that even if you win you can't afford to keep it; you'll still have to sell.'

'Yes,' she agreed, 'but I'll have the money; if he wins I'll have nothing.'

'You still have me,' he said quietly.

Briony looked at him, her face full of remorse. 'I hate hurting you, Paul. I wanted to let you down gently.'

'But you don't love me any more?'

156

Her lips twisted ruefully and sadly and she shook her head. 'I'm sorry, so sorry.'

He was silent for a moment, looking down at his hands on the wheel, then he started the car and they moved on, but Briony had no idea where they went. She didn't think Paul knew either. They stopped at a country pub for their lunch and their conversation was stilted and infrequent, and afterwards he took her home.

'Just remember, Briony,' he said softly, 'that I'll always be here if you need me.'

'I don't think I'm going to tell Nicholas yet that it's all over between us,' she said.

He looked surprised, but said softly, 'That's up to you. In fact I'll still call you and we can still go out if you like, if it will help?'

His generosity made Briony feel even worse. 'That's very kind of you, Paul.'

'I'm being purely selfish,' he admitted. 'Let's say I'm not giving up hope yet.' He leaned across and kissed her and there was more to his kiss than any he had given her lately.

She flung her arms around his neck. 'Paul, I don't know what to say.'

'There is nothing to say—except that I hope we'll always be friends?'

'Yes, yes, of course.' And in that moment she actually felt that she loved Paul. How he could be so understanding after the blow she had dealt him she did not know. He did not deserve it.

She got out of the car and stood watching until he was out of sight down the drive, then turned and marched resolutely into the house. There was a lot she had to say to Nicholas Grant.

As usual he was waiting for her. Not in the hall—he was upstairs—but immediately he heard her footsteps on the tiled floor he came down, his eyes narrowed and thoughtful on her face as if trying to read the outcome of her time spent with Paul.

'You have a nerve,' she spat, 'hinting to Paul that you and I are going to get married. How dare you?'

His dark eyes widened in protest. 'I said no such thing.'

'Not in so many words,' she agreed, 'but it was the impression you gave, and don't try to deny it. Paul wouldn't have told me if it wasn't true.'

'I think your friend Paul is labouring under a mis-apprehension,' he replied. 'Why would I want to marry a girl who doesn't love me?'

'You tell me,' she yelled. 'No, don't bother, the reason's obvious.

He looked at her disparagingly. 'We're back to the old chestnut, are we? You think I want this house so much that I'd marry you whether love was involved or not.'

'Can you deny it?' she flashed.

'Categorically.'

'Then why did Paul get that impression? What did you say to him?'

'Search me,' he answered easily.

'Oh, come on, you must remember what you said.'

He lifted his shoulders. 'I may have said I'd go to any lengths to get the house, but——'

'There you are, then,' she cried, 'and as you've taken me out at least twice to his knowledge you must have known what conclusions he'd draw.'

'You can't blame me for that.' He looked not in the least disturbed. 'What happened today? Is it all over, this—er—friendship of yours?'

'No, it certainly is not,' she lied angrily. 'It would take a bigger man than you to split me and Paul up.'

'He didn't mind me taking you out?' he asked incredulously.

'Of course he minded but Paul's a very forgiving sort of person.'

'He certainly must be,' Nicholas growled crossly. 'You make him sound like a saint. Unless he knows he'd never get another girl to put up with his casual treatment. I'm disappointed in you, Briony, truly I am.'

She lifted her shoulders in an indifferent shrug. 'I don't care what you think. You've made nothing but trouble since you came here and, as far as I'm concerned, the sooner the whole thing is sorted out the better. Thank goodness Richard Brent will be back tomorrow.'

'And still the will hasn't been found,' he said grimly. 'I presume you've made a thorough search?'

'Naturally.'

It was the way that he said it that made Briony look at him with suspicion. 'You don't still think that I have found the will and destroyed it?'

'It is always a possibility.'

'You swine!' she spat. 'Maybe you would do something underhand, but I certainly wouldn't.'

'Then you tell me where it is.'

'I don't know,' she cried. 'You've searched all the bookcases?'

'Yes.'

'The attic?'

'Hell, no.'

'Neither have I,' she told him. 'I think we should look there, today, before we see Richard Brent.'

He nodded. 'But you needn't trouble yourself—I'll do it.'

'In case I find it before you do and pocket it?' she flashed. He really was hateful at times, so obnoxious, in fact, that it was difficult to see how she could ever be attracted to him.

'I didn't say that.'

'But I've no doubt you thought it,' she snapped. 'We'll look together, thank you very much. What's to stop you *planting* a will?'

His eyes widened. 'How can you even think such a thing?'

'Quite easily,' she snapped.

'But I would never——'

'And neither would I do anything underhand,' she cut in icily. 'I don't take kindly to anyone thinking I would do anything criminal.'

'The will has to be somewhere.'

'Maybe James had a safety deposit box that even Richard Brent knew nothing about?' she suggested.

'The bank concerned would have known,' he said confidently. 'It would have come to light when he died. But you're right—we should search the attic. I can't think why I didn't think of doing it before, except that it's not the sort of place I would expect my father to put a will. Let's go look now.'

Briony would have liked to change into her jeans but she did not want Nicholas getting there ahead of her so she followed him upstairs to a little-used part of the house. At the end of a dark passageway was a narrow, short, steep staircase, at the top of which was a door leading through to the attic. It was easy to miss in the gloom and Briony had only ever tried the door once when James was alive. It had been locked and she had never tried it again.

Now, surprisingly, the door creaked open. The attic was much bigger than she had imagined, two bare electric light bulbs revealing years of dust over trunks and boxes. Even the cobwebs were dusty.

'Mind where you're walking,' Nicholas warned her. 'Part of it's boarded, but not all. Keep to the beams.'

They began their search systematically, opening boxes, peering under cloths draped over old lampshades and toys and books. 'Look, here's my old rocking-horse,' exclaimed Nicholas in glee, 'and my lead soldiers—these actually belonged to my father. I had to be very careful with them.'

They were still in excellent condition, noted Briony. They had probably become collector's items. The whole area was full of treasures, even an old Singer sewing machine that must have been one of the first made.

'I had no idea all this stuff was here,' she said. 'It looks as though your father never threw anything away.'

'But it makes our task more difficult.'

She frowned at the reproach in his voice. 'If you ask me, James hasn't been up here. Nothing's been touched for years.'

'Nevertheless, it has to be searched,' he said firmly. 'I have to make very sure.'

'Because you're close to realising that you'll never be able to lay claim to this house?' She eyed him coldly and belligerently. 'Why don't you give up?'

'Never!' he growled. 'I don't care what you say, I don't care if the will isn't found; Thornton Hall belongs to the Thorntons.'

'We'll see what Richard Brent has to say about that,' she answered icily. 'As far as I'm concerned, this second will doesn't exist and *I* am the legal owner.' Her chin came up and she turned around to head back to the doorway, but she was so uptight that she did not look where she was going. One moment there was a solid floor beneath her feet, the next it gave way and she felt herself falling.

In vain Briony tried to grab on to the beams to save herself; she heard Nicholas call out her name in horror— and all in slow motion, amid a cloud of dust and plaster, she crashed to the floor below. Every bone in her body jarred and although she was conscious she lay there in a crumpled heap, winded, afraid to move, wondering how badly she was hurt.

'Briony.' Within seconds Nicholas was down on his knees beside her. 'Briony, can you hear me?'

She was tempted to feign unconsciousness, see what his reaction would be. It would suit his purpose if she had killed herself. The house really would be his then.

'Hell, Briony, speak to me.' There was genuine concern in his voice, his hands gentle as he touched her face.

Briony could keep up the pretence no longer. Her lashes fluttered open and she looked into a pair of worried dark eyes.

'Thank goodness,' he breathed, and he cradled her face as though she meant everything in the world to him.

Briony closed her eyes again and let her thoughts run riot. Everything became brilliantly clear, as though the fact that she could have lost her life in this fall made her see things differently. It wasn't hatred she felt for this man—she had it all wrong; it was love. *Love*! She loved him; she loved Nicholas Grant Thornton.

She had fought love and denied it, but in the end it had won, and at this precise moment Nicholas was acting as though he loved her too, though she knew he didn't. His was nothing more than natural reaction. He would have been as concerned for anyone who'd had an accident.

'Briony!' His tone was urgent now. 'How badly are you hurt? Can you move?'

She looked at him and managed to roll on to her back and lift her arms experimentally. But when she tried to straighten her legs she winced in pain. 'Lord, they hurt,' she cried.

She had come down in one of the unused bedrooms, and Nicholas fetched a pillow and put it beneath her head and covered her with a blanket to keep her warm. 'Lie still now; don't try to move again. I'm going to phone for an ambulance.' His expression was grim and concerned and he actually looked reluctant to leave her. 'You'll be all right for a minute or two?'

Briony managed a weak smile of assurance. There had been no pain to begin with, nothing but a feeling of numbness, now every bone in her body hurt. What an idiot she had been, flouncing away from him like that. Why hadn't she watched where she was going? He had warned her; she should have known. How could she have been so stupid?

Transcending the pain, however, was her discovery that she loved Nicholas. It was a crazy, ridiculous thing to happen. She ought to have seen the warning signs; she ought to have guessed. She would have to be extremely careful now not to give in to him, not to let him win, not to let him get his hands on the house. She would have to make very, very sure that she did not let her heart rule her head.

He was back in no time at all, kneeling on the floor beside her, heedless of the dust and debris on his expensive black trousers. 'How are you feeling?' His voice was anxious, his face full of solicitude, almost as though he blamed himself for what had happened.

'I'll survive,' she said with a wry twist of her lips.

'The ambulance shouldn't be long.'

'I feel such a fool.'

'It wasn't entirely your fault,' he said softly. 'I shouldn't have been so harsh, then you wouldn't have felt the need to rush away.' He touched her face again, stroking gently. 'You could have killed yourself.'

'And then the house would have been yours.'

His tenderness was replaced by a sudden frown. 'That's a rotten thing to say, Briony. Hell, what sort of a guy do you think I am?'

'You once told me that whatever you want you usually get.'

'But not at the cost of someone's life,' he returned firmly. 'Haven't you any idea how I felt when I saw you disappearing like that?'

'I don't imagine you were half as worried as I was.' She managed a faint smile. 'To think, a few feet that way and I'd have fallen on the bed. Trust me to make a mess of it. Could I have a drink of water, Nicholas? My throat's full of dust.'

But before he could get it the ambulance arrived and in no time at all she was on her way to hospital, Nicholas following in his car.

Only one tibia was fractured, they told her after the X-rays, but she had extensive bruising both internally and externally, and they were going to keep her in for a few days' observation.

After her leg was set she was taken, to her surprise, to a private ward where Nicholas sat waiting for her. 'What's all this?' she asked, indicating the comfortable room.

'It's because I want to be able to sit and talk to you with a modicum of privacy.'

'I'm sure that's not necessary,' she announced a trifle tetchily. She was angry that he had money to throw around like this when she had none, when Thornton Hall was her only asset and he was desperate to take it from her. The love she felt for him did not alter the fact that he still annoyed her intensely at times. This was one of them.

'How are you feeling?' he asked, dismissing the subject of the room as though it was of no interest at all.

'The truth?' she asked with raised eyebrows. 'I can't find anywhere that doesn't hurt.'

'I'm actually surprised you've got away with so little injury,' he told her. 'You had a lucky escape.'

'You call this luck?' she jested, indicating her plastered leg.

'Honey, if I could I'd take your place. Look, I have to get back now; Jojo will be wondering where I am.'

His daughter had been out when the accident happened and Briony could understand his concern. Or was it because he felt he had now done his duty and wanted to get back to the Hall? To continue his search, perhaps? It was futile loving this man whose sole interest was in bricks and mortar.

The kiss he gave her was brief but infinitely sweet all the same, tingling through her veins, exploding through her nerves, setting her whole body on fire—as if she hadn't enough to cope with!

She was actually troubled by her feelings for Nicholas. She had never thought it would happen. He was her enemy, after all; how could she possibly love him? But she did, there was no escaping the fact, and if the truth were known she would be quite happy living with him at Thornton Hall for the rest of her life.

Who the legal owner was would not matter if Nicholas loved her as well, but she knew this would never happen, so she had to fight these feelings, resist them, deny them, keep them hidden, never, ever let Nicholas know how she felt.

He would be so triumphant. His gamble would have paid off. It was what he had set out to do right from the beginning, the only way he could get his hands on the house if the will wasn't found. He was despicable; she ought to hate him. She gave a deep sigh. How closely hate was related to love. At first she had been unable to distinguish between the two, and, now she had, it made things even more difficult.

For the next hour or so Briony drifted in and out of sleep and then woke suddenly to find Paul standing beside her bed.

'Hello,' she said faintly, adding foolishly, 'What are you doing here?'

'I've come to see you.' He was deadly serious, not a hint of a smile on his lips.

'But—how did you find out?' After all, she had only left him a few hours ago; he wouldn't have phoned her in that short space of time.

'Nicholas Grant rang and put me in the picture,' he announced.

Briony's surprise showed on her face. 'He did?' This was the last thing she had expected Nicholas to do.

'I guess the man has a heart after all.'

Evidently, thought Briony, though this was the first sign she'd seen of it. 'What did he say?'

'That you'd fallen, that you were in hospital, that he thought I should know, considering we're going to get married. I didn't disillusion him.' This last was added with a wry twist to his lips, and his blue eyes were sad as he looked at her.

'Thank you,' she said huskily, and she felt dreadful that she had scarcely thought about Paul since she'd been in here.

'So what happened?' he asked, pulling up a chair. 'Nicholas didn't give me any details.'

When she told him he looked shocked. 'I'm surprised you weren't more careful.'

'I was angry. Nicholas Grant could try the patience of a saint.'

'And yet you love him?'

'No!' she denied, then added reluctantly, 'Maybe, I don't know, I'm not sure.' She could not hurt him further by admitting that she did love Nicholas, unreservedly.

'I wish I could believe you feel nothing for him,' he said quietly. 'It's worried me constantly since we parted. I should hate you to get hurt, Briony.' His hand came down over hers on the bedclothes. 'I've known you so long that I feel you're a part of me; if you get hurt I shall be hurt too.'

'Paul.' She picked his hand up and held it to her cheek. 'I won't get hurt, I promise. I've got my eyes wide open.'

He leaned closer to her and she thought he was going to kiss her, until a harsh voice interrupted them.

'I'm sorry to intrude on this touching little scene.'

'Nicholas!' Briony looked at him in surprise. 'I didn't expect to see you again today.'

'Obviously.'

'Thank you for letting Paul know that I'm here.'

'It's my pleasure,' he clipped drily. 'I've brought some of your night-clothes. Hospital gear is never very becoming.'

Briony flushed at the thought that he had been going through her drawers, and he saw and guessed. 'Jojo sorted them out,' he informed her coolly. 'I'll just leave them here so that you can get on with your cosy tête-à-tête.'

He walked swiftly out of the ward, and although Briony wanted to call him back she did not do so. She felt it would tell Paul all too clearly that she loved this other man.

'He's thoughtful,' said Paul, 'unless it's all an act because he's still trying to get the house off you.'

'Nicholas is an enigma,' she told him. 'I don't think I'll ever understand him. Half the time he's ruthless and selfish and another time he can be as nice as pie. Let's not talk about him.'

Paul stayed for another hour, but in the end he said he must go.

'From one sick-bed to another?' she asked with a rueful smile. He had told her that his mother was still not feeling well.

'I'll call in some time tomorrow,' he promised her, 'although it will probably be fairly late because I have to go to Leicester.'

'You don't have to put yourself out,' Briony told him.

'It's not putting myself out to see the girl I love.'

She wished he hadn't said that; she felt uncomfortable. He had surprised her yesterday when he had apparently given her up with good grace; now he was spoiling it by being unusually possessive. 'I'll look forward to seeing you,' she said softly, though perhaps not very convincingly.

She slept fitfully, woken at intervals by nurses taking her temperature and blood-pressure, and giving her routine bedtime drinks which she didn't want, until finally all became quiet, and she drifted into a much deeper sleep.

The next morning she was woken early and her aches and pains were, if anything, worse. She half expected Nicholas to come and see her and was disappointed when the whole day went by and she saw nothing of him. Paul came and went and bedtime came round again and she felt really angry that Nicholas was ignoring her.

And then on Tuesday morning at about eleven he came. He strode into the ward wearing his black leather jacket and black, close-fitting trousers. When he asked the nurse who had been talking to her for coffee she ran away immediately to do his bidding. She had been unable to take her eyes off him, and Briony guessed that she would be telling all her colleagues about the dishy man visiting Briony Weston.

'You're looking better,' he said, sitting down.

'I guess I feel all right, considering.' She kept her tone cool, but inside a fire had been lit, every sense come alive. She had tried so hard not to think of her love for this man, told herself that it was all a figment of her imagination, and yet now he was here she knew it wasn't. She craved for him to touch her, for a kind smile, a caress, but no, he was polite but distant.

'How much longer are they going to keep you in?'

Briony shrugged. 'I'm waiting for the doctor to come and give his verdict. Another day at the most, I would think. Apart from my leg, and extensive bruising, I feel fine.'

He nodded. 'Good. I've been to see Richard Brent.'

James's solicitor had gone completely out of Briony's mind, and now she groaned inwardly. Damn her accident. She had wanted to go herself, or at the very least with Nicholas, so that she could make sure he didn't put any pressure on this old family friend. 'What did he say?' she asked, her voice coming out breathless, as though she had run a four-minute mile.

'He was indeed astonished to see me.'

'I bet he was. Did he recognise you? You must have changed quite a lot in eighteen years.'

'He did not recall me instantly, I have to confess, although he did say afterwards that my face was vaguely familiar and he knew he ought to be able to place me.'

'And what did he have to say?'

'About the will?'

Briony nodded.

'He has no knowledge of it.' The confession was made discontentedly, a brooding frown adding to the harsh angles of his face.

'So what's the position as far as the house is concerned?'

His mouth was grim. 'It's legally yours.'

Briony gave the glimmer of a smile. 'And I can kick you out any time I like?'

'I'm afraid so.'

She felt a sneaking satisfaction, though not as much as she had expected. 'Did you finish searching the attic?'

He nodded. 'Without results, though I did find something of interest. In fact I was quite stunned. You'll have to wait until you come home to see what it is, though.'

Although Briony was curious, she said nothing. If he wanted to play games then let him. The wonderful part about it all was that he couldn't take Thornton Hall from her. 'Did you show Richard Brent your father's letter?'

'Of course.'

'What does he think?'

'The same as you—that he never got around to making another will.'

Briony would dearly have loved to say, 'I told you so', but when she saw the disappointment on his face, the dejected bow to his shoulders, she actually felt sorry for him. She wanted to tell him that it didn't matter, that he and Jojo could live there just the same, but that would be letting him win. Far better to let him stew while she decided what to do. He deserved it after the way he had treated her.

'Finding out that the house is still mine is the best news I've heard in a long time,' she said. 'In fact it's brilliant news. If it weren't for this darned leg I'd get up and do a dance.'

His eyes narrowed on hers. 'You'll be glad to see the back of me?'

'What do you think?'

He didn't answer. 'Will you still sell, or will you and Paul make Thornton Hall your home?'

Briony pretended to give the matter some consideration. 'I think I shall probably sell. It's a bit too big really; it takes a lot of looking after. Besides which, I know Paul wouldn't be happy there.' Which was the truth. He had always said he wouldn't like to live at the Hall.

'In that case I have a proposition to make. I'd like to buy it from you.'

CHAPTER TWELVE

BRIONY could not believe what she was hearing; no, that was wrong—she could believe it, but how Nicholas had the audacity to make such a suggestion she did not know. He had turned up with some cock-and-bull story about another will, had tried to force her out of Thornton Hall, had tried to get the house from her by any method he could, and now, because he hadn't got anywhere, he was offering to buy it.

If he had done so in the beginning she would have thought far more of him, might even have suggested they share; instead he had done everything to turn her against him. And this latest offer was the final straw. It added insult to injury, and if she had been strong enough she would have taken great pleasure in kicking him out.

'You can't be serious?' she asked at length.

'Indeed I am.'

'You're a swine, do you know that?' Her tone was bitter, her eyes hard.

Nicholas frowned, as if unable to understand her reaction. 'Why do you say that when you're going to sell the house anyway?'

'Because, although you must have been prepared to buy it all along, you thought you'd try and get it for nothing. God, I hate you.'

'You misinterpret my motives, Briony. Offering to buy Thornton Hall is a last resort. It's not something I ever planned to do. There is, of course, another solution.'

Her brows rose and she looked at him scornfully. 'Something else equally devious, I've no doubt.'

171

'You could marry me. That would solve both our problems.'

Briony felt her heart begin to race. It would be the perfect solution—*if only he loved her*! But no way was she going to marry a man just so that he could live in Thornton Hall and call it his own. Talk about a marriage of convenience; it was a ludicrous proposition. She shook her head from side to side.

'Is that a no?' he asked quietly.

'It means I'm just too flabbergasted for words. How could you possibly suggest such a thing?'

'It seems a very logical arrangement.'

'And you think it would work, marriage without love?' she asked coldly. 'Or wouldn't that side of it interest you? Is owning Thornton Hall of more importance? Marrying me would certainly save you a lot of money, wouldn't it?'

'Money is of no concern,' he answered with a shrug of his wide shoulders.

It never was, to those who had it, she thought, and yet he had tried his hardest to get the house without handing over any cash. She was thankful that she had stuck it out, that she hadn't given in to soft-hearted emotions. He was a cold, cunning, conniving bastard and no mistake. He had pushed and pushed right to the very end. 'Damn you, Nicholas Grant,' she grated. 'Why the hell don't you get out of my life?' Apart from all her other aches and pains, her head began to throb, and she wanted nothing more than to be able to lie down quietly and forget this conversation altogether.

'Thornton Hall has always been my home,' he said succinctly. 'And the way I see it, there are only the two choices left.'

'Sell to you or marry you?' she concluded viciously. 'Both of them stink.'

'Why?' There was a narrowed intentness to his eyes as he watched her, a slight flaring of his nostrils, a muscle jerking in his jaw.

'I'll tell you why,' she spat. 'Selling to you would be as good as giving in. And I won't marry you for the same reason. I've fought you this long, Nicholas Grant; I'm certainly not backing down now.'

For several long seconds he said nothing, watching her closely, face impassive, eyes probing. At length he spoke. 'You hate me that much?' The tone of his voice lacked feeling of any sort. It suggested acceptance, reluctant acceptance.

'You've not given me any reason to feel otherwise,' she replied, her eyes meeting his, not giving anything away either. 'Admittedly we get along all right sometimes——' *very well, in fact, sometimes too well*! '—but on the whole we've done nothing but fight like cat and dog. Why should I let you have what you want?'

He lifted his shoulders. 'You don't have to, of course, but the offers for Thornton Hall are not exactly streaming in. If you won't marry me, if selling is a more attractive proposition, then I'll even give you more than you're asking.'

'You're very magnanimous all of a sudden,' she derided.

'You leave me no choice. You're a very hard woman, Briony Weston.'

'It's a case of having to be,' she said. 'I've no one else to look after me.'

'You have Paul. If he was a man with any backbone he'd be doing all this for you.'

Briony ignored his derogatory comments. 'I thought you were interested in buying back your father's company. Are you so wealthy that you can do both?'

An eyebrow quirked. 'The way I look at things, Normac is a very profitable company; I don't think I'd be living on the breadline.'

'If you were you'd never survive,' she jeered grimly. 'You can't possibly have any idea what it's like having to count every penny.' Suddenly she was tired of fighting him, and knew that the pain of unrequited love would become unbearable. 'I give in; you can buy the house—lock, stock and barrel—on one condition.'

'And that is?'

'That you don't throw me out straight away, that you'll give me time to find somewhere else to live.' Even as she said the words she knew it was foolish. She was hanging on to him, clinging, hoping, wishing that he would return her love. She should know it would never happen, not now, not if it hadn't already. Lord, they had spent enough time in each other's company to know how they felt about each other. Nicholas's feelings were selfish, as always; he only ever thought about number one.

'You can stay as long as you like,' he said. 'Forever, if you wish.'

Briony's fine brows rose. 'Another generous gesture. Why?'

'Maybe I don't want to lose you.'

A faint spark of hope, dismissed instantly. 'You were prepared to kick me out if the will was found.'

'I never said that, Briony.'

'Not in so many words,' she agreed, 'but it was the impression you gave. Thornton Hall was all you wanted, despite having walked away from it eighteen years ago.'

'I would still never have kicked you out.'

Briony eyed him warily. 'I'm sorry, but I don't be-lieve you, and it doesn't really matter anyway. I shan't prey on your generosity for any longer than is absolutely necessary.'

'Paul might suggest you move in with him and his mother.'

'I don't get on with Mrs Holman,' Briony said tightly.

'Is that so?' A faint smile lifted the corners of his mouth. 'It sounds as if it will be one hell of a happy marriage—a wimp like Paul for a husband and a disapproving mother-in-law. You'll be well blessed.'

'As a matter of fact,' she said, 'I'm not going to marry Paul.' The moment the words were out she regretted them—she hadn't even meant to say it, couldn't think why she had.

The faintest of frowns settled on Nicholas's brow. 'You're not?'

'No.' It was almost a whisper and she wished she could slide down between the covers and pretend not to be there.

'When did you change your minds? When he came to see you on Sunday? Did Paul reject you at a time like this? Damn the man, has he no conscience? Wait till I——'

'It wasn't like that,' Briony interrupted hurriedly. 'We—er—never did make any definite plans. I let you think it, but——'

'Hell, Briony, what are you saying?' He got up from his chair and walked round to the other side of the bed, looking down at her, his eyes dark and puzzled. 'You never were going to marry Paul?'

She shook her head. 'He did suggest it, when he came back from his seminar, but—I said no.'

A gleam lit Nicholas's eyes and he spoke slowly and thoughtfully. 'Was there any particular reason why?'

'I guess I realised that our relationship had gone sour,' she confessed quietly and reluctantly.

'Then there is no reason why you can't marry me?' Still the dark eyes were intent upon hers, and he leaned lower over the bed. 'Except that you don't love me?'

His voice had gone husky and sent a tremor of feelings through Briony's body.

She did not answer; what could she say? How could she tell him the truth when his feelings for her were non-existent, when his marriage proposal was completely mercenary?

'You must be aware that when we're not arguing about the house we're completely compatible?' he went on. 'You can't dispute that fact. Thornton Hall has been our only bone of contention. With that out of the way there's no reason why we shouldn't live happily together, no matter that love isn't a major part of it. Who knows what will develop, given time?'

Was he giving her a hint that he might learn to love her? That his feelings were more than she had hoped for? There was certainly no disputing their physical responses to each other, but was he now suggesting that these feelings could grow into something more on his part?

An elation began to grow inside her that she found difficult to control; her lips quivered and trembled until finally they burst into a radiant smile.

Nicholas's straggly brows rose. 'What thoughts are going on inside that pretty head of yours?'

Briony bit her lower lip in a sudden bout of shyness. 'That—er—perhaps you might be right.'

'Is that a yes, you will marry me?' He began to smile too and his hands came down on the bed on either side of her, his face inches from hers.

'It's a maybe,' she admitted softly.

'Perhaps this will persuade you to turn your maybe into a yes,' he murmured, his mouth descending.

The lightness of his kiss made it all the more erotic, the merest brushing of his lips over hers, the faintest touch of his tongue, inciting emotions, making her want to respond, making her want to hook her arms behind his head and pull him closer, only the extent of her aches and pains stopping her—and the fact that she could be giving too much away! Even if she did agree to marry him it was too soon to open her heart, to let him see that she did in fact love him, much too soon.

He drew back and looked at her expectantly, hopefully. 'Well?'

'I'll give it some serious thought.'

A frown drew his thick brows together. 'How long am I expected to wait?'

'Until I get home,' she said.

'Which might be today. Maybe I should go find that doctor?' He straightened, but still looked down at her, and Briony found it difficult to read his expression.

He looked pleased, but was it pure pleasure or was it triumph? Was she doing the right thing? Ought she to say no now and done with it? Ought she to take the money and run? Oh, God, how could she answer these questions? How could she discern good from evil? He was a clever man, used to getting his own way. Was she playing right into his hands? The trouble was she loved him so much, and living with him would be infinitely preferable to all the money in the world. She closed her eyes.

Instantly he was all concern. 'You're tired?' he said. 'I've exhausted you? I'm sorry.'

But she knew he wasn't and she looked at him with a faint smile. 'I think you should go.'

'I think I should wait for the doctor.'

'No, I'll ring you if I want you to fetch me home.'

'You promise?'

'Yes.'

With that he had to be satisfied.

When he had gone Briony's mind was in a whirl. It certainly wasn't the ideal marriage proposal, but it was better than moving out of Thornton Hall—which she had never really wanted to do—and losing Nicholas altogether. The love she felt for him had put a whole new perspective on things. Her pride had gone by the board, and even the fact that she knew his proposal was purely mercenary did not bother her.

Although she had asked for time she knew she was going to say yes. It was insane, totally out of character for her to even contemplate such a drastic solution, but she wanted Nicholas with a desperation that amazed her.

It was the following day before Briony was allowed home. Nicholas had telephoned her several times but he hadn't been to the hospital again and she was acutely disappointed.

When he turned up to collect her she did not let him see the joy that she felt, maintaining a cool façade, hiding the sizzling sensations that shot through her when he helped her into his car. It was not his low-slung sports car, which would have been difficult with her leg in plaster, but a more sedate black BMW with plenty of leg-room.

'Where has this come from?' she asked as she settled inside.

'Hired for the occasion,' he told her. 'I thought it would be more comfortable.'

'You're very considerate; I didn't expect it.'

'I'm not entirely the ruthless swine you keep calling me.' He slipped in beside her, the powerful engine little more than a purr as he drove steadily out of the hospital grounds, careful to avoid any bumps which might cause her pain.

'I've seen very little of your other side.' The car was full of his presence and for an instant she felt irritated by this power he had over her. It was making her act out of character, taking over her life. She was on the threshold of promising to marry him. What could be crazier than that, considering their circumstances?

'Then that's something I shall have to remedy.'

And it would be easy now that he was almost sure of getting his own way, she thought.

'I have your lunch ready,' he said as they neared Thornton Hall. 'I hope you're hungry?'

'Starving,' she admitted, wondering how long he would look after her like this.

As Jo was at college they had the house to themselves, and the beef bourguignon he had put in the oven was totally delicious. He really was an excellent cook.

No mention at all was made during their meal of his unusual marriage proposal, but afterwards, when he suggested they go into his father's study, Briony knew the time had come for her to give him her answer. This was the place where all serious decisions were made.

She declined his offer of a steadying arm and used her crutches instead, fiercely hanging on to her last bit of independence.

On James's desk was a file that she had not seen before. 'What's that?' she asked.

'Sit down and have a look,' said Nicholas with a curious smile.

She obeyed, and inside was a sheaf of letters tied together with a piece of narrow yellow ribbon. Briony frowned and looked at him.

'Read them,' he said.

She spread them out on the table and to her astonishment saw that they were all the letters that Nicholas had sent to his father in the early years—letters pleading to make amends—and, what was more amazing, James's answers, written, but not posted, pouring out the older man's heart, his love, his sorrow, begging his son's forgiveness.

Tears welled in Briony's eyes long before she had finished. If only James had posted these letters it would have made such a difference. He would possibly still be alive now. Their whole life would have changed.

'Oh, Nicholas!'

He nodded, his lips clamped together, his face pained.

'It's so cruel. Poor James, poor you. It need never have been.'

'I had no idea,' he said, his voice gruff with emotion.

'I wonder why he didn't post them.'

'Pride; stubborn, cussed pride.' His tone grew stronger. 'We're both of the same mould. We're both as much to blame, but at least I know now how he felt. I wish he could have known that I wanted to make amends too.'

'Perhaps he does,' said Briony softly.

'I hope so. I hope he's up there watching over us. He would approve of you and me getting married, Briony, I know he would. Have you made up your mind?'

Up until that moment she had still been wavering, but now she found herself nodding. 'I'll marry you, Nicholas.' Her heart thumped like a wild thing as she said it and she hoped and prayed that she wasn't making a huge mistake.

She wasn't sure whether it was joy or relief that crossed his face; whatever, he came to her and lifted her carefully to her feet, holding her to him, gently, as though she were very precious. 'You've made me one very happy man,' he said.

Briony could not help thinking that it was because he had now very nearly got his hands on Thornton Hall— and without paying a penny. Was she a fool? Would she lose everything in the end? She prayed not. She loved this man and wanted to be with him for all time. She would make him love her, she would.

They told Josephine when she came home and the girl was at first shocked and then warily pleased. During the last week she had come to accept Briony and they were gradually building a much better relationship, but Briony could see that the girl was still not altogether sure that she approved of their forthcoming marriage.

Nicholas was all for an immediate wedding, but Briony wanted to wait until her leg was mended. 'I'm definitely not getting married with my leg in plaster,' she told him.

He accepted it reluctantly and in the days that followed he spent much of his time probing into the Camerons' affairs, finding out as much as he could about Normac, prior to putting in his preliminary offer for the company.

Charles Cameron had, of course, no idea yet that Nicholas was back in the country. 'He'll have the devil's own shock when he finds out,' Nicholas said to her, 'and the first he hears of it will be when I put in my bid.'

'You won't tell him who you are?'

'Perhaps not,' he agreed. 'I'll play him at his own game and do it all through a third party. But he'll find out in the end, believe me.'

There were days when Briony spent a lot of time alone. Not that she minded; she actually enjoyed the time to herself to sit and think, to wonder at what the future held in store. Occasionally she felt like backing out of it all, and then Nicholas would come home and he would hold her and kiss her, and her love would well and she knew that she would never change her mind.

Her minor bruises had cleared up, leaving only her fractured leg to cause problems. She had grown quite adept on her crutches, however, and got about quite easily, until one day she managed to hook one of them around the hall table and went crashing to the floor.

She wasn't hurt, but she lay still for a moment, gathering her wits. From her recumbent position she could see the underside of the table and, sticking down from behind one of the drawers, right at the back, was an envelope.

Curiously she fished it out and saw that it was addressed to Richard Brent. But it wasn't sealed—the flap wasn't even tucked in—so she peeped inside, and her heart went bump when she realised that it was the missing will. She could not stop herself then; she withdrew the sheet of stiff paper and her eyes flicked over the contents.

> To my son, Nicholas, I leave Thornton Hall and all its contents, on condition that he lets my wife, Patricia, and her daughter, Briony, carry on living in the house for the rest of their lives. If they wish to move on then part of the estate is to be sold to finance their needs.

There were further minor bequests, much the same as they had been in the original will, but none that affected her like this. She felt sad. There would be no need now for Nicholas to marry her. She had always known that his reason was to get his hands on the Hall, even if she had sometimes told herself otherwise.

She was very tempted to destroy the will to save her own happiness, but her conscience would not let her do so, and when Nicholas returned an hour or so later she silently handed it to him, watching his face carefully as he read it. But no expression entered the planes of his face, or delighted the darkness of his eyes. There was nothing, nothing at all to tell her what he was thinking. She decided to speak first.

'You won't have to marry me now; the house is yours.'

'Where did you find this?' Still his face was deadly serious.

'Stuck at the back of one of the drawers in the hall table. It must have slipped inside, and your father forgot all about it. He might even have thought he'd posted it to Richard Brent; he always used to put his post on that table.'

'It doesn't make sense to me,' said Nicholas.

'Sense or not, the situation now is very clear,' she said determinedly.

He frowned. 'You mean you still think that the reason I wanted to marry you was to get my hands on the house?'

'Well, wasn't it?' she snapped. 'You came to me in the hospital and said you wanted either to buy the house from me or marry me. What was I supposed to think?'

He clamped his lips together, a shadow of annoyance on his harshly sculpted features. 'Sit down, Briony; we need to talk.'

'As far as I'm concerned, there's nothing to talk about,' she rasped. 'Everything is perfectly clear. I shan't stay on, of course; I'll find myself some lodgings somewhere and——'

'Briony, you're talking nonsense.' His tone was sharply angry. 'This has changed nothing. I still want to marry you; I still want you to be my wife.'

She looked at him cautiously. 'You do?'

'Of course I do. Hell, Briony, I'm no mercenary. My reasons for wanting to marry you are the same as anyone else's. I love you, you idiot.'

Briony gasped and swallowed hard. 'You do?'

'Yes, I do,' he assured her. 'The only reason I didn't tell you was because I didn't want to embarrass you, myself as well. You've no idea how painful it is to love someone who doesn't love you in return. I thought that if I could persuade you to marry me, then—in time— you would learn to love me too.'

Briony stood with her mouth open, unable to take in what he was saying. 'You—actually—love—me?'

'Is it so difficult to accept?' he asked, his tone deeply emotional.

'As a matter of fact, yes,' she managed to whisper. 'I cannot believe it. You've never given me any indication.

I thought it was pure animal attraction. I thought the house was your prime interest.'

'Maybe I've said that,' he admitted, 'and maybe I've even thought it, but, hell, you're worth more to me than a thousand Thornton Halls put together.'

Briony's heart was beating in double-quick time. It was all too much to take in. Nicholas loved her! He truly loved her. It was beyond comprehension. She sank awkwardly down on to a chair, her leg stuck straight out in front of her.

Nicholas immediately dropped down to his knees and took her hands in his. 'I'm sorry if I've distressed you.'

'You haven't,' she said swiftly, shaking her head. 'I'm a little bemused, that's all.'

'Maybe I should have told you before.'

'I think you should have,' she said.

'I didn't want to frighten you away.'

'With love?' she queried. 'Oh, Nicholas.' She raised his hands and pressed them to her mouth, and she was frowning, as though in pain.

'What is it, honey?'

'Haven't you any idea?'

He shook his head.

'I love you too.' It was a softly worded confession, barely audible.

He jerked upright and looked at her disbelievingly. 'Briony, is this true?'

She nodded.

'But for how long? Since when? Why didn't you tell me?'

'The same reason as you didn't tell me,' she replied with a grimace.

'When did you discover it?'

'When I fell and broke my leg,' she confessed shyly. 'It all became shatteringly clear. I always thought it was hatred I felt; it wasn't until then that it suddenly struck me that I loved you.'

'Hell, I panicked that day when I saw you disappearing,' he groaned. 'Is that why you agreed to marry me, because you loved me, not because you couldn't bear losing Thornton Hall?'

She nodded.

'When I offered you the choice of marriage or selling, If you chose the latter I was actually banking on you loving it too much to leave. I couldn't bear the thought of losing you. It was a last resort, but not in the way you were thinking.'

'I would have left,' she said, 'if I had sold.'

'Then I'd have lost,' he said quietly. 'Actually it's still your house, Briony.'

She frowned and looked at him. 'What do you mean?'

'This will was never witnessed; it's not valid. He began to laugh as he spoke and Briony laughed too, and in no time at all they were both helpless with laughter. Until he kissed her! Then it all became serious. It was their first kiss in the knowledge of mutual love; it was a promise of things to come, of a greater understanding of each other.

Seconds slipped into minutes, happy minutes, love-filled minutes. 'If only my father were alive now,' Nicholas said at length when they finally found the strength to let each other go. 'He would be so happy for us both.'

'He truly would,' she agreed.

'Do you know,' he said, 'at this moment I'm even prepared to forget what Charles Cameron did to my family. With you by my side, who cares about the past? It's the future that matters. Me and you, always, forever. Us, our children, their children. Many more generations of Thorntons living at the Hall. It's a dream I had when I was living in America, a dream I never thought would come true. But now it has, and it will. I love you, Briony; I love you with all my heart.'

'And I love you just as much, Nicholas. This is a moment I also thought would never happen.'

'Oh, Briony.' He held her close again and their hearts throbbed in unison and Briony knew, deep down in her heart, that this was how it was going to be. They would be one, a team, living at Thornton Hall, raising their children, filling it with happiness and love for the rest of their lives.

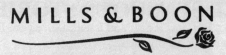

RELENTLESS AMBITIONS, SHOCKING SECRETS AND POWERFUL DESIRES

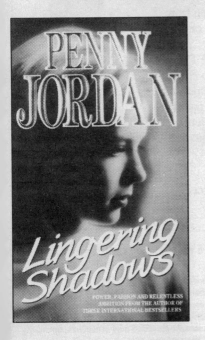

Penny Jordan's stunning new novel is not to be missed!

The dramatic story of six very different people— irrevocably linked by ambition and desire, each must face private demons in a riveting struggle for power. Together they must find the strength to emerge from the lingering shadows of the past, into the dawning promise of the future.

W❂RLDWIDE

AVAILABLE AUGUST 1993   PRICED £4.99

Accept 4 FREE Romances and 2 FREE gifts

FROM READER SERVICE

Here's an irresistible invitation from Mills & Boon. Please accept our offer of 4 FREE Romances, a CUDDLY TEDDY and a special MYSTERY GIFT!
Then, if you choose, go on to enjoy 6 captivating Romances every month for just £1.80 each, postage and packing FREE. Plus our FREE Newsletter with author news, competitions and much more.

Send the coupon below to:
Mills & Boon Reader Service,
FREEPOST, PO Box 236,
Croydon, Surrey CR9 9EL.

NO STAMP REQUIRED

Yes! Please rush me 4 FREE Romances and 2 FREE gifts! Please also reserve me a Reader Service subscription. If I decide to subscribe I can look forward to receiving 6 brand new Romances for just £10.80 each month, post and packing FREE. If I decide not to subscribe I shall write to you within 10 days - I can keep the free books and gifts whatever I choose. I may cancel or suspend my subscription at any time. I am over 18 years of age.

Ms/Mrs/Miss/Mr _____ EP55R

Address _____

_____

Postcode _____ Signature _____

mps
MAILING PREFERENCE SERVICE

Next Month's Romances

Each month you can choose from a wide variety of romance with Mills & Boon. Below are the new titles to look out for next month, why not ask either Mills & Boon Reader Service or your Newsagent to reserve you a copy of the titles you want to buy – just tick the titles you would like and either post to Reader Service or take it to any Newsagent and ask them to order your books.

Please save me the following titles:		Please tick √
THE WEDDING	Emma Darcy	
LOVE WITHOUT REASON	Alison Fraser	
FIRE IN THE BLOOD	Charlotte Lamb	
GIVE A MAN A BAD NAME	Roberta Leigh	
TRAVELLING LIGHT	Sandra Field	
A HEALING FIRE	Patricia Wilson	
AN OLD ENCHANTMENT	Amanda Browning	
STRANGERS BY DAY	Vanessa Grant	
CONSPIRACY OF LOVE	Stephanie Howard	
FIERY ATTRACTION	Emma Richmond	
RESCUED	Rachel Elliot	
DEFIANT LOVE	Jessica Hart	
BOGUS BRIDE	Elizabeth Duke	
ONE SHINING SUMMER	Quinn Wilder	
TRUST TOO MUCH	Jayne Bauling	
A TRUE MARRIAGE	Lucy Gordon	

If you would like to order these books in addition to your regular subscription from Mills & Boon Reader Service please send £1.80 per title to: Mills & Boon Reader Service, Freepost, P.O. Box 236, Croydon, Surrey, CR9 9EL, quote your Subscriber No:................................... (If applicable) and complete the name and address details below. Alternatively, these books are available from many local Newsagents including W.H.Smith, J.Menzies, Martins and other paperback stockists from 10 September 1993.

Name:...

Address:...

....Post Code:..........................

To Retailer: If you would like to stock M&B books please contact your regular book/magazine wholesaler for details.

You may be mailed with offers from other reputable companies as a result of this application. If you would rather not take advantage of these opportunities please tick box ☐